ACCLAIM FOR THE WORKS OF MICHAEL CRICHTON!

"Michael's talent outscaled even his own dinosaurs of *Jurassic Park*. He was the greatest at blending science with big theatrical concepts. . .There is no one in the wings that will ever take his place."
—*Steven Spielberg*

"Crichton keeps us guessing at every turn."
—*Los Angeles Times*

"[Crichton] marries compelling subject matter with edge-of-your-seat storytelling."
—*USA Today*

"Crackling. . .mysterious . . ."
—*Entertainment Weekly*

"One of the great storytellers of our age. . . What an amazing imagination."
—*New York Newsday*

"Crichton writes vividly."
—*Washington Post*

"Compulsively readable."
—*National Review*

GRAVE DESCEND

MICHAEL CRICHTON WRITING AS JOHN LANGE™

MICHAEL CRICHTON

WRITING AS JOHN LANGE™

GRAVE DESCEND

BLACK STONE PUBLISHING

Printed in the United States of America

ISBN 979-8-200-98704-7
Library of Congress Control Number: 2022948555
Fiction / Mystery & Detective / General

Version 1

CIP data for this book is available
from the Library of Congress

Blackstone Publishing
31 Mistletoe Rd.
Ashland, OR 97520

www.BlackstonePublishing.com

www.MichaelCrichton.com

FOREWORD

by Sherri Crichton

It is such an honor and pleasure to see the John Lange books freshly and newly published by Blackstone, to reintroduce these books to fans and also present them to a whole new generation of readers.

My husband, Michael Crichton, put himself through Harvard Medical School in the sixties by writing pulp fiction novels. He wrote them as John Lange and Jeffery Hudson before he was published under his own name with *The Andromeda Strain*.

The John Lange books are adventure stories, and you can start to see in them the genius that would, only a few years later, become so apparent. While later in his career Michael made a point of separating his identity from these novels, I suspect he had a lot more affection for them than he showed.

The books are set in the late sixties and seventies and were his tribute to Ian Fleming's James Bond novels and to one of his favorite Alfred Hitchcock films, *To Catch a Thief*; the books are about secret treasures, heists, archaeology, unlikely heroes, seductive and at times treacherous lovers, classic villains, and much more.

I look at these John Lange novels with great affection as I picture Michael studying medicine day and night and writing these fun books over school breaks and holidays. Becoming an author was his dream—not being a doctor—and the John Lange novels truly are a testament to his exotic imagination, places he dreamed of visiting, and above all, they show the birth of Michael as an author.

In an interview from December 2000, Michael shared details of the beginning of his career in the sixties. His comments reveal how he went from John Lange to Michael Crichton:

I was one of those kids who seemed to know very early what I wanted to do. I was driven to writing. I did a lot of it starting around the third grade, when I wrote this enormously long puppet show that had to be typed up by my father with carbon copies so that all the kids could have their parts.

At that time most of the third graders were writing a page, and I had written this very long thing. But I just wanted to do it. I don't know how to explain it any differently.

When I was thirteen or fourteen, I had visited a place in Arizona called Sunset Crater Volcano National Monument; I thought it was extremely interesting and relatively unknown. I complained that people didn't have more knowledge about this place, and my mother and father told me, "Well, why don't you write an article?" I said, "I can't do that." And they said, "No, no, the *New York Times* accepts articles in their Travel section from all kinds of people." So I wrote an article and they published it.

I'd read that only two hundred people in the United States were able to support themselves full time writing books. I thought to be one of two hundred people in the entire country seemed a very difficult group to join. And six thousand doctors graduated every year. That seemed much more doable. But while I was in medical school, I began to write to pay the term bills. I wrote under a pseudonym because the grades you got in those days were very dependent on the evaluation of your teachers, and I was quite convinced that if they knew I was running off to write books, they would think less of me.

The names I chose were John Lange and Jeffery Hudson. John Lange, I drew from my own first name, which is John, and I thought of these books as James Bond thrillers, fairy tales for adults. I associated the books to Andrew Lang, who was an author of Victorian fairy tales, and Jeffery Hudson, who was a little person from the court of Charles I of England and a great adventurer. I thought it would be very entertaining for me to have the name of a little person since I am six nine.

The book I wrote under the name Jeffery Hudson, *A Case of Need*, was optioned for a movie and eventually made by Blake Edwards. It made my life very strange because I was sometimes going to California to talk to the screenwriter, then I'd come back and put on my whites to be in the hospital. There's a bizarre difference between being an impoverished student and then having these periods where I got into limousines and drove around Hollywood. It made me a little crazy. Yet, even when *A Case of Need* won the Edgar Award for Best Mystery and I had to go down to New York to accept the award, no one in the medical school ever found out, which was odd. It showed me how self-centered the institution of medicine really was.

Eventually, I was going to write a nonfiction book, which ultimately was published as *Five Patients*, and I had to go to the dean to get permission to skip certain classes to do this book. He said, "Well, writing a book is very difficult. Do you realize how difficult it is? Have you ever done anything like that?" And at that point I finally thought it was okay, and I said, "Yes, actually, I've written several books."

My next novel to be published was *The Andromeda Strain*; I wrote it in secret, and when [director] Robert Wise bought it to make it as a film, it got publicized that there was this kid in medical school who had sold a book to the movies for a lot of money.

My picture was on the wire services. The story was officially out. Everybody knew. But looking back on it, it was a very free time.

GRAVE DESCEND

He is no wise man that will quit a
certainty for an uncertainty.
—SAMUEL JOHNSON

PART I
SWIFT SHIP

Much may be made of a Scotchman,
if he be caught young.
—SAMUEL JOHNSON

1

Starting in the early dawn light, he had driven up into the mountains, leaving the flat sprawl of Kingston behind him. He had cut through the tiny mountain villages, the native huts perched precariously beside the road; then down through lush valleys of tropical vegetation, damp in the misty morning wetness; and finally up once more to the cold air of the peaks which sheltered the north coast.

Now it was eight o'clock in the morning, and he was coming down, hunched over his bike, doing a hundred, with the sound of the engine in his ears, and the wind in his hair. In the distance, he could see blue water, with waves breaking across the inner reefs, and hotels lining the beachfront. A momentary glimpse: then he plunged into the final twisting green decline which led him to Ocho Rios.

McGregor hated Ocho Rios. Once a beautiful and elegant strip of coastline, it was now a long succession of gaudy hotels, ratty nightclubs, stud services, and steel-band discos, all patronized by hordes of vacuous tourists who were seeking something a little more expensive but no different from Miami Beach.

It was to serve such tourists that the Plantation Inn had been built, an enormous complex on twenty acres of lavish grounds, phony colonial buildings, restaurants, and snack bars. It was shielded from the road by a high fence. There was a guard in khakis at the gate, a smooth-faced native man who saluted each limousine of tourists as it arrived from the airport.

The guard did not salute McGregor, however. Instead, he held up one hand, and rested the other on the butt of his holstered gun.

"You have business here?"

McGregor stopped, idling the bike. "I'm seeing Mr. Wayne."

"Mr. Who?"

"Wayne. W-A-Y-N-E."

The guard checked the guest register on a clipboard, made a mark against one name, and nodded. "Keep the noise down," he said, as he stood aside to let McGregor pass. "The guests are sleeping."

McGregor smiled, gunned his bike, and roared noisily into the compound. He passed manicured gardens, beds of bright flowers, carefully watered palms. At length he pulled up in front of the main hotel building, which was only three years old, but carefully constructed to resemble an old Jamaican plantation.

He parked the bike and went into the lobby. At the front desk, the clerk in a red jacket and tie stared at his greasy dungarees and dirty blue pullover. "May we help you, sir?" he asked, with an expression that was intended to be a smile, but was closer to a wince.

"Mr. Wayne."

"Is he, uh, expecting you?"

"Yes, he is uh expecting me," McGregor said.

The man winced a little more. "Your name, please?"

"James McGregor."

The clerk picked up the telephone, dialed, and spoke quietly for a moment before hanging up. He was clearly displeased, but managed to say, "Take the elevator to the right. Room four-two-three."

McGregor nodded, and said nothing.

Despite the early hour, Arthur Wayne was up and dressed, sitting at a small table on which breakfast had been laid out. He was a lean man in his middle fifties, with a severe face and gray, cold eyes; despite the casual resort atmosphere, he wore a three-piece pinstripe suit.

"Sit down, McGregor," he said, buttering his toast. "You made good time. Want some breakfast?"

"Just coffee," McGregor said. He lit a cigarette and sat in a chair near the window. "How'd you know where to reach me?"

"You mean, at your . . . friend's?" Wayne smiled, and poured a cup of coffee. "We have our ways. I didn't really think you'd be here so fast, though."

"I told you, eight thirty."

"Yes, but we called at six, and it's four hours from Kingston to Ocho—"

"Not the way I do it."

"Clearly," Wayne said. "Clearly." He bit into the toast and glanced over at McGregor. A businessman's glance, steady, appraising. "You're older than I expected."

"So are you."

"How old are you, anyway?" He set down his toast, and started on the scrambled eggs. "Tell me a little about yourself."

"There's not much to tell," McGregor said. "I'm a

diver. I'm thirty-nine. I've lived in Kingston fourteen years. Before that I did salvage work out of New York and Miami. It didn't pay, and I hated it, so I came down here."

"And before New York?"

"I was in the Pacific, clearing beaches for the Marines."

Wayne chewed his eggs. "What was that like?"

"Like a bad dream." McGregor puffed on the cigarette, and stared out of the window. He disliked this part: the early establishment of credentials with the client. You had to put on a good show. He hoped Wayne wouldn't get onto the leg business.

"I heard you were injured in the war," Wayne said.

"Yes. Nearly lost a leg. It took the medics three years afterward to get it back together."

"Remarkable," Wayne said, still chewing. "Remarkable. Well, I won't beat around the bush, Mr. McGregor. You come highly recommended to us. We're very eager to have you."

McGregor smiled slightly. "Especially since I'm the only one on the island equipped to do the job?"

"We are more concerned," Wayne said, "about finding the right man for the job."

"But your alternative is flying in a team from Florida or Nassau, and that costs. It costs plenty—all that heavy equipment."

"Are you telling me you're raising your rates?" Wayne said.

"Just thinking about it."

"I won't beat around the bush," Wayne said. "This is an important, very delicate job. We'll pay you anything you ask, within reason."

"Depends on the job."

"Then let me tell you," Wayne said, wiping his mouth with a napkin, "about the job."

He pushed away from the table, and, coughing slightly, lit a cigarette. He reached for a large briefcase and opened it, taking out maps, charts, and marine blueprints, which he spread across the floor.

Then he picked up a glossy photograph of a ship, and handed it to McGregor.

"This is the problem," he said. "The yacht *Grave Descend*. One hundred twenty-three feet at the waterline, luxury fittings, five staterooms, each with bath—"

McGregor said, "Tonnage?"

"Forty-four twenty, I think."

"You think?"

Wayne checked his papers. "Yes . . . forty-four twenty."

"Where did it go down?"

"Five miles east of here, and three-quarters of a mile offshore, give or take. According to the best estimates, it's about here"—he gave McGregor a marine chart—"just outside the outer reefs. There's two reefs here, an inner reef of about twenty feet, and an outer reef that falls off to—"

"I know about the reefs," McGregor said. "When did it go down?"

"Yesterday."

McGregor paused. "Yesterday?"

Wayne sucked on his cigarette, and smiled. "You're wondering why I am here so soon. Marine insurance companies aren't usually so punctual in sending a representative—isn't that what you are thinking?"

"Roughly."

"I think you will understand as time goes on. The boat is insured for two million ten, so we are understandably concerned, but that is only part of the problem."

McGregor frowned. He had never heard of a marine insurance rep calling a ship a *boat* before. And Wayne was remarkably disorganized. He looked again at the map. "How does she lie?"

"We're not sure. We think the bow faces north, toward open water, and that the stern rests here. That would put the stern in about sixty-five feet, and the bow in about eighty. The drop-off is quite sharp here—"

"Fragmentation?"

"No. As far as we know, not. It is, we hope, intact."

"But you don't know."

"No. We don't."

McGregor frowned. "Whose is she?"

"She belongs to an American industrialist who made his fortune in steel. He bought it from an Australian nine months ago, and kept it in the Mediterranean until a few weeks ago. He brought it across to Miami—West Palm, actually, to a marina there—for repairs, and then had it sailed here."

"He wasn't aboard?"

"No. He lives outside Pittsburgh, and was planning to fly down, and take her from Ocho down to Aruba."

McGregor nodded. "And you want me to tell you if it can be raised?"

"Among other things," Wayne said. "But we have an additional concern, of great importance to us, from the insurance standpoint."

"What's that?"

"We want to know why it went down in the first place," Wayne said, and stubbed out his cigarette.

———

There was a short silence. McGregor waited for an explanation; when none came he said, "I'm not sure I follow you."

"I'm not sure I'm making much sense, myself," Wayne said. "You see, something happened aboard that boat. There was an explosion—in the engine room, according to all accounts. The boat was outfitted with twin six-hundred-horsepower Caterpillar diesels—"

"Diesels?"

"Yes, why?"

"Go on."

"Twin six-hundreds. She cruised very nicely at fourteen knots. Those diesels were thoroughly checked out at West Palm. They were in perfect running order. Yet there was an explosion. And the boat sank very swiftly. It was down in a matter of minutes."

"Anybody hurt?"

If there had been a death or serious injury, it would be out of McGregor's hands. The Jamaican government would conduct its own inquiry, since the boat had sunk in Jamaican territorial waters.

"No," Wayne said. "That's the strange part of it. There were six crew members, including the skipper, Captain Loomis. And there was one passenger. They all made it off the boat safely, and were picked up by a local fishing boat."

"I see. Where is Captain Loomis now?"

"Here in town. He's staying at the Hotel Reserve."

McGregor nodded. He knew the Reserve, a cheap hotel back in the hills, where yacht owners traditionally put up their crews.

"I'd like to talk to him."

"Of course. I'll arrange it for later in the day—"

"Don't bother," McGregor said. "I'll do it myself."

Wayne shrugged. "As you wish."

"And the passenger? Who was he?"

"She, actually," Wayne said. "Monica Grant. Captain Loomis did very well as far as that was concerned."

"How do you mean?"

"I mean publicity." Wayne picked up the day's copy of the *Daily Gleaner*. "Not a word about the yacht and its sinking. Not a blessed word. Captain Loomis managed to keep everything quiet, and a good thing too."

McGregor said nothing.

"You see, the owner of the *Grave Descend* is quite a good friend of Miss Grant. And the owner's wife . . ."

"Okay," McGregor said. "Got you."

"So there you have it," Wayne said. "The ship went down, and we don't know why. The owner is extremely eager to keep it quiet, and he doesn't want Miss Grant's name mentioned."

"You can't hope to conceal it forever," McGregor said.

"No. No, we wouldn't even try. What we intend is to announce the sinking as occurring this evening. That will allow us to safely remove Miss Grant from the scene of the action, away from the reporters and photographers. It is, after all, a very good story—bizarre sinking of a luxury yacht, with mysterious, beautiful girl on board. A good enough story to make the Pittsburgh papers."

"Miss Grant is beautiful, is she?"

Wayne shrugged, and walked onto the balcony. "Have a look for yourself." He pointed down to the pool. "The blonde in the deck chair, reading the magazine."

McGregor looked down at a girl in a small bikini, lounging at the poolside.

"Beautiful." He nodded.

"She's registered as a guest of the hotel now," Wayne said. "She will have been registered for fully twenty-four hours before news of the sinking is released. No one will connect her to it."

McGregor frowned. "You seem," he said, "to be going to great lengths to protect the owner of this ship. Isn't that a little beyond the call of duty for an insurance agent?"

"I suppose," Wayne said, "but the circumstances are special."

"How's that?"

"The owner, Robert Wayne," he said, "is my brother."

———

He let that sink in. McGregor didn't know exactly what to make of it, but he would decide later. Meantime, there were other problems.

"About money . . ."

Wayne said crisply: "We are prepared to offer you a hundred a day."

"Plus expenses," McGregor said.

"Yes. Plus expenses."

"I'll need a decent-size skiff, say thirty feet. Compressor, tanks, equipment—I have all that, but it goes on a per diem basis of a hundred dollars."

Wayne nodded. "All right."

"And my own rate is two hundred a day," McGregor said.

At this, Wayne paused. "I was given to understand," he said, "that you did not run quite so high—"

"I don't usually," McGregor said. He tapped the marine chart showing the position of the *Grave Descend*. "But this is powerhead country."

"I beg your pardon?"

McGregor smiled slightly. "Powerhead country. It means you don't go down there without a gas gun and a powerhead shaft. Especially outside the far reefs."

"I'm afraid I still don't—"

"Because," McGregor said, "that stretch of coast is the furthest Atlantic tip of the island, the most unprotected water. It's thick with hammerheads."

Wayne looked confused.

"A kind of shark," McGregor said. "One of the worst kinds."

"I see."

"Two hundred a day," McGregor said.

Wayne nodded. "Two hundred it is."

"I'll take care of getting the skiff, and paying the man. I'll have all my equipment over here by . . . by tomorrow morning."

"Very good."

"We can begin then."

"All right. You'll want something to get you started," Wayne said, and quickly wrote out a check for a thousand dollars, waved it dry, and handed it to McGregor. "Is that sufficient?"

"I think so."

"And I was going to suggest that perhaps later in the day you might want to fly over the site. We can charter an airplane quite easily from the Ocho airfield. Perhaps at two this afternoon?"

McGregor shook his head. "Sun's too high," he said. "You won't see shadows at two. Better three thirty or four."

"All right. Shall I arrange it?"

"Yes."

"Then we'll meet at the airfield?" Wayne said.

"Fine," McGregor said, and left, check in hand. He went down to the lobby, exchanged sneers with the desk clerk, and walked out to the pool to talk with Monica Grant.

2

Up close, she was very beautiful indeed, judging from what he could see of her, which was practically everything. The bikini was very small; her body was lithe, darkly tanned, and relaxed.

"Miss Grant?"

She put down her magazine, setting it across her brown abdomen. She saw his clothes and frowned. "Yes?"

"I'm Jim McGregor." She continued to frown. "The diver," he explained.

"Oh yes. How are you?" She held out her hand, and replaced the frown with a smile. It was quite a nice smile. He noticed that she had green eyes.

"Are you going to raise the ship?"

He sat down on the concrete deck next to her,

and lit a cigarette. "Well, I don't know. But we'll soon find out."

"I hope you can," she said. "It's a beautiful ship. The most beautiful I've ever seen."

McGregor said, "If you have a few minutes, I'd like to talk to you about it."

Another smile: "Of course."

"Where did you board her?"

"In West Palm. I flew down from New York after the ship finished its repairs. I wanted to get some sun before Robert arrived. He was supposed to meet us here, you see. We were going to have a beautiful cruise down to Aruba. Robert was even talking of going to Venezuela."

"Venezuela?"

"Yes. But I don't know if he was serious or not. Robert likes to talk about big plans."

"I see. So you boarded in West Palm. When was that?"

"Two weeks ago," she said. In response to his questioning look, she said, "I'm a dancer. Until recently I was working in the Copa. But I quit when Robert suggested this trip . . ."

McGregor nodded. She looked like a dancer. "Two weeks ago would make it the second?"

"That's right. The second of November."

"And who else was aboard?"

"Captain Loomis, and the crew. Five other crew members. I was a little worried about that, but they were very polite."

"Where did you sail from Palm Beach?"

"To Bimini. Captain Loomis said he wanted a shakedown cruise. He didn't seem very confident in the boat, for some reason. So we went to Bimini, and stayed overnight, to take on supplies."

"Supplies?" McGregor thought she must mean fresh water; the trip from West Palm to Bimini was too short to require anything else, and Bimini was an expensive port for most other supplies; a wise captain would wait for Nassau or Freeport.

"Yes. There was some furniture and things, for the cabins."

"Furniture?"

"Yes. So we picked that up, and went on to Nassau."

"The trip was uneventful?"

"Yes. We had one cloudy day, that was all."

"No mechanical trouble?"

"We never had any mechanical trouble," she said, "right to the end."

"And from Nassau . . ."

"We went to Jamaica directly. No stops. It was perfect weather, just delightful. And we arrived in Jamaica three days ago."

"Where did you pass customs?"

"Customs?"

"Yes. You had to pass Jamaican customs at your first port of call."

"You mean where the little inspector came and asked if we had firearms and stuff?"

"That's it."

"In Ocho," she said. "Right here."

"This was your first stop?"

"Yes," she said.

McGregor nodded. "Go on."

"Well, we went to the . . . east, is it? Yes, east. From Ocho along the coast. We were going to park off the shore near where Robert has his house. He has a house farther along the coast, you see. We were going to stop there and wait for him to fly down. Captain Loomis got us there yesterday afternoon, and we parked—"

"Moored," McGregor said.

She gave him a dazzling smile. "I really don't know much about boats. Yes, we moored offshore. I wanted to go closer but Captain Loomis said there were reefs, we couldn't go any closer than we were. So we anchored there, and I spent the rest of the afternoon in the sun. And then suddenly I was in the water, and the ship was sinking. Just like *that*!" She snapped her fingers.

"There was an explosion?"

"I don't really know," she said. "I've been trying to remember it, but it happened so fast . . . I think there must have been an explosion, at least some kind of noise. And the next thing, I was in the water, and Captain Loomis was getting us away because he said there was suction around a sinking boat, and I started to get scared then. It was very scary. I would have been more scared if I really knew what was happening, but I didn't; I was dazed."

"No one was injured by the explosion?"

"No. That was lucky. Captain Loomis was very worried about it all. When the fishermen picked us up, he paid them a lot of money—a hundred dollars each—to keep quiet. I didn't understand what the fuss was, until later. Then I understood that Robert had given him instructions about me. Robert's worried about his wife, you see. She has all the money, and he's worried she'll divorce him."

"So you were picked up by fishermen," McGregor said. "What time was that?"

"I don't know. About six. It was starting to get dark. We were taken ashore and we went to Robert's house. We found clean clothes there—even a dress for me—and suitcases and stuff, and Captain Loomis had us all check into hotels. And he called Robert's brother in Chicago, the insurance man, who flew down last night. He's very nice—have you met him?"

"Yes," McGregor said.

He frowned.

"Is something wrong?" Monica said.

"No," he said. "Nothing."

———

Walking back to his bike, he lit a cigarette and tried to put things together. Something wrong? Christ, nothing was right. He ticked off the points in his mind:

Wayne. If he was really a marine insurance investigator, he was either very inexperienced, or very dumb.

The charts. The position of the ship had been marked by a cross. Normally, a presumed site was located by a broad circle, as much as a quarter of a mile in diameter. Never a cross—never so exactly.

The story. Granted that Monica Grant was an exceptionally attractive girl, even granted the need to keep the sinking out of the Pittsburgh papers, how did one keep it out of the Jamaican papers? Jamaica was a large island in some ways—one hundred and fifty miles by fifty miles, with Kingston the largest English-speaking port south of Miami—but in other ways, it was small. News traveled fast and irrepressibly. The *Daily Gleaner* was a small, eccentric, but proud newspaper, with a reputation for reporting everything worthwhile that happened on the island. How had Loomis managed it?

How could you keep the sinking of a luxury yacht a secret, even for twenty-four hours?

It seemed impossible. But then, in his fourteen years on Jamaica, McGregor had done quite a bit of salvage work, and he had heard enough stories to go with wrecks to realize that anything was possible. Especially in the realm of stupidity. Men wrecked boats who had never sailed before; they wrecked them by putting them into reverse when they thought it was forward; they wrecked them by not paying attention to charts ("A chart? You mean those map things?"); they wrecked them by getting drunk and falling asleep at the rudder; they wrecked them by letting the ships drift while they played games with girls in staterooms . . .

Every story was different, and they were all, to his ears, improbable. But not like the *Grave Descend*. That was not merely improbable; it was weird. Even the name of the ship was weird. He had meant to ask Wayne about the name of the ship.

No matter, he thought. He would ask the captain, Loomis.

3

The town of Ocho Rios was nothing much. An intersection, a couple of gas stations, a few bars and tourist shops, and you had passed it all. The organization of the town was simple and straightforward: a road ran along the coast, cut into the hills which climbed high from the beaches. On the coastal side of the road were the hotels, the money, the polish, the tourists. On the mountain side of the road were the native quarters, the huts and shacks and naked children.

And the Hotel Reserve.

The Hotel Reserve was a two-story frame building, painted pink, and flaking. In a way, it had its own dilapidated charm, but McGregor knew that it was pure business inside. The top floor was rented out to yacht crews; the ground-floor rooms were kept vacant, so that the studs who picked up women in the bars downtown could bring them back for a quick taste of local rhythm.

He parked his bike and went inside; he was directed upstairs, to Loomis's room. He knocked, and a grumbling voice said, "Who the hell is it?"

McGregor waited, saying nothing. After a moment, he knocked again. There was a pause, and Loomis opened the door a crack.

"Yeah?"

"My name's McGregor. I want to talk to you about the *Grave Descend.*"

"What about it?"

"I'm the diver."

"Oh."

Frowning, Loomis opened the door wider. He was a burly man wearing undershirt and shorts, smelling of whiskey. The air in the room was stuffy as McGregor entered.

It was a simple room, with only the expected furnishings: bureau with cracked mirror, washbasin, dilapidated bed, tired-looking black girl in the bed.

Loomis turned to the girl. "Beat it, sweetie," he said. "Time to go."

The girl started to dress. Loomis ignored her, going to a small table on which sat a bottle of rum and two dirty glasses. He poured himself a shot and gulped it back, shivering.

"Ugh," he said, staring out the dusty window at the children playing in the street below. "Hell of a way to wake up. What'd you say your name was?"

"McGregor."

"Good to know you, McGregor," Loomis said, extending a damp palm. They shook hands. "Want a belt?"

"No thanks," McGregor said.

"Hell. Do you good." He poured two shots, and gave a glass to McGregor. "Bottoms up."

The girl finished dressing, putting on a shiny green dress, very tight. She paused at the door.

"Talk to you later, sweetie," Loomis said. "Now beat it."

She left. Loomis sighed and sat on the bed. "Christ," he said, "I feel awful. You talk to Wayne?"

"Yes."

"Nice fella. He didn't say all the things he could have said. Very practical fella. You know, it's a hell of a mess. One roaring hell of a mess. But Wayne didn't give it to me."

He took a long swallow of the rum.

"I'll tell you though," he said, scratching his stubbly chin, "I'm worried about one thing. Guys like Wayne, real nice and polite, they can get you, know what I mean? Like the way I figure it, they need me now. They really *need* me. So they're pleasant, right? But when they don't need me anymore . . ." He shrugged, finished the drink, and poured another. "Drink up," he said.

McGregor took a sip of the rum. It was raw and thick, very cheap.

"I don't mind telling you," Loomis said, "I'm plenty scared. I blew it, and I'm scared."

"How's that?"

"Well, the owner, Robert Wayne, gives me a call in West Palm. Long-distance call. And all he has to say is that nothing better go wrong—and particularly, nothing involving the girl. Now I know a little about the guy, and I know his position, right? He's supposed to be this big steel executive, but that's horseshit. He makes maybe sixty, seventy thou—which is okay, but it doesn't keep you in yachts or stuff like Monica. You need like two hundred thou for that. So where's it come from? His wife, I figure. His wife has the bread and he's scared she'll find out he's hustling these chorus girls, so he calls me, long distance, to make sure no word gets out."

Loomis sighed and shook his head.

"So I tell him, real confident, that no, nothing will happen, just relax. I tell him, and he says okay, fine, and hangs up. Then the next day, the girl arrives. You seen her?"

"Yes."

"So you know why the hell old Wayne doesn't want his moneybags wife to get wind of her. Newspapers dig up some picture of her in a bikini and it's all over, man. All over. Goodbye, two hundred thou."

McGregor nodded.

"So anyhow, the girl shows up, and we take the boat out. I wanted to—"

McGregor said, "Did you bring it across the Atlantic to West Palm?"

"No, no. That transatlantic stuff is big time, they got a special crew to do it. The boat used to be Australian, you see. Australian flag. It was built in Japan in 1961, and sold to some guy in Sydney. Then Wayne bought it last year, and had it shipped to the Mediterranean. He kept it in Monte Carlo or someplace, used it for entertainment and so on. Changed the name."

"It's an unusual name."

"Damned spooky name, you ask me. *Grave Descend.* That's a hell of a name for a ship. But you know what it is, it's what all these new guys do with ships. Give them screwy names. You see those powerboaters in Miami, they name their ships *Wet Dream* and *Sea Pussy* and stuff like that. Think it's funny."

"You took command in West Palm?"

"Right. I'm not doing much there, managing a little overhaul for one guy or another, and I get this offer to skipper a ship for a guy in Pittsburgh. He wants me to put together a crew and run him down to Aruba, or maybe Venezuela. I say what the hell, sure. The price is right too, let me tell you. Damned generous price."

"You'd never seen the ship before?"

"No. It came in from Naples. That was its last port before coming over. Had a little outfitting done, some nice gold fixtures, and some huge goddamned sculpture in the main stateroom. Modern sculpture, all chrome. Then it was brought over here, and I picked it up."

"And repairs were made?"

"Well, no, not repairs. We just checked it out. It was overhauled in Naples, they did a fine job. We just checked it out."

"When did you sail?"

"The second of the month. We were supposed to be down here on the eighteenth, you see, and I wanted plenty of time, in case we had a snag. We went to Bimini, a kind of shakedown, getting the feel of things, putting the crew together—"

"The crew was new too?"

"Yeah. Miami boys. You can always get a crew in Miami. Mostly the old lifeguards, too old to work the stud business, they crew out."

"I see."

"So we went to Bimini, and we picked up some ballast—"

"Ballast?"

"Yeah. Funny thing, the ship was listing some to port, not much, but it was off. So we trimmed her up and went on."

"Why was it listing?"

Loomis shrugged. "Just the personality of the boat, you ask me. They're all a little different."

"And from Bimini?"

"Nassau. Supplies, food, water, stretch the crew's legs. We were going very fine, and came directly down to Mo Bay."

"Montego?"

"Right. Had customs there, no problems—"

"You passed customs in Montego Bay?" McGregor said.

"That's right. Why?"

McGregor said, "Nothing."

"It was logical. First port, and they're better equipped at Mo Bay than Ocho. Hate to wait around for customs, you know, just waiting there for some damned uniformed flunky."

"How long were you in Montego Bay?"

"About six hours. Then we sailed east to Ocho, and arrived two days ago. Yesterday we went farther east to Silverstone. That's about five miles east of Ocho; it's a promontory, you may have seen it. House out there that Mr. Wayne owns, called Silverstone. We were supposed to anchor there and wait for him. He was going to fly down at the end of the week."

"And?"

Loomis took another drink. "Christ, I don't know. I swear I don't know. We were running that ship beautifully. The crew was careful. Nobody was smoking belowdecks—in fact, the guy I put on the engines didn't smoke at all, he was a nonsmoker. But somehow it happened."

Loomis finished his drink and poured himself a still larger slug.

"I'm forward, on the bridge actually, when it happens. I feel the ship rock—sort of jump—and I hear the sound. It wasn't very loud, like a rumbling, but it must have blown out the stern or maybe half the underplates because right away she started to go down. The people on the stern, like Miss Grant—she was sunbathing on the stern—they were knocked into the water. The rest of us on board were going to throw them life preservers when we realized just how fast the boat was going. It was really going fast. But peaceful, you know. Like a rock settling in."

"What did you do next?"

"Well, look, I'm no hero. I got the hell off. Besides, it was going so fast, I was afraid it would suck the others down, they didn't know anything about moving off from a sinking ship. I managed to get everybody clear, and the ship went. Stern first, but it was all pretty fast."

"And then?"

"Then we made for shore, doing the best we could. A fishing boat saw us and picked us up. I paid the boys off pretty good. By then I was thinking, you see, about what had happened, and what it all meant. I decided to get smart. I took everybody up to Silverstone, got them into fresh clothes. We took the car at the house and drove into town. I put the girl into a hotel, and the crew here. And then I called Arthur Wayne."

"Why him?"

"Owner's instructions. On the phone, Robert Wayne says to me, 'Anything goes wrong, don't call me, call my brother Arthur in Chicago.' So I did."

"And he flew right in?"

"Boy, did he," Loomis said. "Came in by private jet last night. And he right away figured out what to do."

"About the wreck?"

"About the girl. He knew we'd have to report it sooner or later, so he figured out this plan where we'd report it today."

"I see."

"I get the crew together, and we go out there about five o'clock, and swim ashore, and call the cops. Pretty neat, huh?"

"But someone must have seen the ship go down yesterday."

"Not out there. It's a pretty deserted stretch. Only people that know are me and the crew, the girl, the two fishermen, the maid at Silverstone, and the hotel people here. And they've all been paid. Pretty well too."

"Very neat."

"You're telling me. Only one thing bothers me: once this is all over, what happens?"

"How do you mean?"

"I mean," Loomis said, "what happens to me? I got them into this big fix, and it's real expensive. What're they going to do to me?"

"I don't know," McGregor said.

"Neither do I," Loomis said, "and I'm worried plenty."

4

The Cockatoo was a bar west of town, a shanty where the steel bands played at night, and the locals sang songs about the big bamboo while the lady tourists fluffed their dresses, drank their rum punches, and waited to get picked up. During the day it was dark, cool, and quiet.

McGregor found Sylvie there, leaning against the bar, talking with some of the boys from the band. She wore stretch slacks and a tight blouse; the boys were definitely interested.

McGregor slapped her bottom as he came up. "Hello, love."

She smiled and kissed his cheek. The boys looked envious.

Sylvie was French, originally from Martinique. She had come to Kingston three years before, to study at the university; that was where McGregor had met her. Sylvie was a former Miss Martinique, and she did great things for clothes, particularly tight clothes.

"I just arrived," she said. "How long have you been here?"

"Since eight thirty."

She made a clucking sound. "You drive too fast. What's it about?"

He explained the sinking of the *Grave Descend*. Sylvie wrinkled her nose and brushed her long black hair back from her face. "What an awful name."

"It's an awful story. Everybody trying to cover up for the mistress."

"And they want you to salvage it?"

"I'm not sure," McGregor said. "Because there's a big problem with the whole story."

"What's that?"

"Wayne is spending a lot of money and effort to hoodwink everybody into believing that the ship went down today, not yesterday."

"So?"

"Why did he have to explain it all to me? He could have fooled me like the rest of them."

"Perhaps he wants to be sure you're ready to go first thing tomorrow," Sylvie said.

"Perhaps," McGregor said. "We're going to fly over the site later today . . ."

He paused.

"Is something the matter?"

"No," he said. "I just wondered whether Wayne wanted me *not* to be ready first thing *today*."

"What are you talking about?"

"I'm not sure," McGregor said. "Come on."

———

In Sylvie's sports car, it was a short drive along the curving, mountainous road east of Ocho Rios, past all the hotels, and finally into a rugged and relatively undeveloped stretch of coast. As always, McGregor was struck by the beauty of this region; he wondered regretfully how many years it would be before the hotels extended out here.

"Where are we going?" Sylvie said.

"To Silverstone," McGregor said.

"Whatever for? You're going to fly over it later today."

"I know."

"Then what—"

"It's a lot of little things," McGregor said. "Like the fact that Wayne had a map that marked the site of the wreck. He marked it quite exactly. Most people, when locating a wreck, draw a circle, and say, 'I think it's somewhere in here.' Wayne was more definite. He felt certain where it was, and how it lay, and in what depth."

Sylvie was frowning. "You think he set it up?"

"I don't know." McGregor thought about that, but it didn't make sense. Why should Wayne set it up?

"Then there are other things. Like Miss Grant, who says the ship passed customs in Ocho, and the captain, who says they passed it in Montego."

"She could be confused."

"I'm sure she's confused," McGregor said. "The question is why."

"What else bothers you?"

"The course the boat sailed. It was originally moored in Monte Carlo, but it went to Naples for overhaul before the Atlantic crossing."

"So?"

"From Monte Carlo, a yacht needing an overhaul would most likely go to the harbor in Nice. At most, it would go to Genoa. But why all the way to Naples?"

McGregor took a turn very fast. They were approaching Silverstone now; the road was narrower, less well-paved, with many potholes.

"Then Bimini. Loomis says the ship was listing so he altered ballast in Bimini. It seemed very odd that a boat was trim enough to cross the Atlantic, but not good enough to go from West Palm to Bimini."

"Maybe ballast was shifted in West Palm."

"Or else something was taken off the ship—or put on."

They arrived at Silverstone. It was a high promontory jutting out into the ocean; a white house, secluded in palm trees, was located near the sea; on either side of the promontory were small bays with curved beaches, deserted.

"What do you see?" McGregor said.

"Nothing," Sylvie said.

McGregor smiled. "No conveniently located local fishermen in quaint little boats that just happen to be large enough to accommodate seven extra passengers?"

"You're too suspicious," Sylvie said.

From their vantage point, they could see only the nearest of the two bays; the promontory blocked the farther one.

McGregor drove on down the road, and stopped a second time.

"No," he said, looking out at the ocean, "I'm not too suspicious."

There, clearly visible in the midday sun, riding three-quarters of a mile offshore, was the luxury yacht *Grave Descend.*

5

"It makes no sense," Sylvie said.

"I know."

He reached into the glove compartment, removed a pair of binoculars and, propping his elbows on the door, peered out at the ship. Riding in the offshore swell, the bow was turned to the ocean. Clearly visible on the stern was the name of the ship in black letters. There could be no mistake.

He swept the binoculars along the profile. "No sign of anyone there."

"There must be someone," Sylvie said.

If there were, he would be on the bridge; a skeleton crew always kept a man on the bridge. McGregor peered through the binoculars once more. As the ship rocked

gently, the sun glinted off the windows, making it difficult to see in, but after several seconds he was quite sure.

"Nobody there."

"It's not possible," Sylvie said.

But McGregor was already getting out of the car so
that he could look back at the house. Silverstone was
still obscured by palm trees, but he could get some idea
of the size: it was enormous, a mansion looking out on
the ocean. From the house, a series of stone steps were
cut into the rock, running down the side of the promontory to the beach.

But there was also apparently a pool near the house,
for McGregor saw a fat, pale man bounce on the diving
board and jump into water with a great splash. He could
not see the pool itself because of shrubbery.

He watched longer, hoping for a better glimpse of
the pale man. Robert Wayne was not due to fly down
until the end of the week. Who could it be? Not Arthur
Wayne. He wasn't fat; the profile was all wrong.

Not a servant, surely.

Then who?

He shrugged. It was probably a friend, or a houseguest.
It could be almost anyone; if Robert Wayne could afford a
huge yacht, he could also afford to put up a houseguest. Or
fifty.

He turned his attention back to the yacht. Sylvie came to stand by his side.

"It is very peculiar," she said, "that they would hire you to salvage a yacht which is afloat."

"There's always a first time."

"Well," she said, "at least it will be an easy job." She paused; he looked over and saw her frowning. "Won't it?" She gazed over his shoulder and suddenly pointed. "Look!"

He swung his binoculars back to look at Silverstone. Clearly visible was the fat, pale man at the poolside. He was walking toward the edge of the promontory, near where the stairs to the beach began. He seemed relaxed and unconcerned.

McGregor could not see his features clearly, but it was evident he was not a white Jamaican businessman—even the man's face and neck were pale.

As he watched, the man raised a small box which he was carrying in one hand. He pulled at it in an odd way; for a moment, McGregor did not understand, and then he saw the sun flash on wire.

An antenna.

Radio of some sort. Probably a walkie-talkie.

The man stared toward the yacht. McGregor swung his glasses to look at the boat, but nothing was happening there; it remained, to all appearances, deserted.

Looking back at the fat man, McGregor saw he was not speaking into the box as he had expected. Instead, he seemed to be fiddling with it.

He heard a muffled thud.

Sylvie said: "The yacht!"

Looking back, McGregor saw thin black smoke rising from the stern. The water around the ship churned and boiled, and then was still.

"I'll be damned . . ."

There was no further sound. He continued to watch as the *Grave Descend* sank. It did so slowly and majestically while the man on the promontory watched.

When it had finally disappeared beneath the water, they could still see the swirling and bubbling at the surface, marking where it had gone down.

The man on the promontory watched a few moments longer, then put down the antenna and went back to the house.

"I think this is all very strange," Sylvie decided.

"I think you're right," McGregor said. He got back into the car. "Come on."

"Where are we going now?"

"It's where I'm going. You're going to meet Roger when he brings the stuff."

"All right. And you?"

"I'm taking a plane trip with Arthur Wayne," he said, "to look at a sunken yacht."

———

The airport at Ocho Rios was built for very small planes and very daring pilots. Boscobel airstrip was only three thousand feet long, and the drop-off the end was a great inducement to get up—or down—before you reached the end.

McGregor met Wayne in the small terminal. Wayne pointed to a yellow Piper Cub on the runway. "There she is, ready to go."

McGregor looked at him; Wayne smiled back. He still wore his three-piece suit, despite the heat, and he had a flushed but heavy air of respectability.

This man is a liar and a crook, McGregor told himself as he looked at Wayne, but he had trouble believing it. If he hadn't seen the yacht himself . . .

"Good. Let's get moving."

The trouble, McGregor thought, walking across the hot asphalt to the airplane, the trouble was that it was clearly some kind of setup. He was being played for a sucker. The question was what kind of sucker, and why?

He decided it was time for a small experiment. As the engine started with a grunt and a puff of smoke, and the pilot taxied forward along the runway, McGregor said, "I've been making arrangements for the dive tomorrow."

"Good. Everything going well?"

The plane lifted off, climbing high over the ocean, curving in a slow arc east, gaining altitude as it swung.

"Actually, not so well," McGregor said. "A few snags."

"Oh?"

He gave a chagrined little smile. "I'm afraid my credit's not so good, Mr. Wayne. Everybody seems to want a little more."

"More what?"

"Money," McGregor said.

Wayne's eyes, previously smiling and friendly, turned cold. "How much more?"

"Ten thousand dollars."

"That is not exactly a little more."

"It's what they want." McGregor shrugged.

"What who wants?"

"Everybody. The skiff man. My own people. They're covering themselves, you see. In the past, we've worked on private jobs and when we were finished, the owners disappeared."

"I assure you, Mr. McGregor," Wayne said, "that we will not disappear."

"I know that," McGregor said. "But it's hard to convince the others."

Wayne was silent for a long time. Finally, he said, "I don't believe I like you."

"Well, I'm not in love with you either."

"I find your story unconvincing. I think you're trying—"

"Look, if you don't like it, get yourself another boy."

"But there is no time," Wayne said, "as you are quite aware. We have counted on you."

"Inside forty-eight hours, you could have divers and equipment flown in from Nassau."

"That is not the point. The point is that you agreed—we agreed—on an arrangement and you were paid what you felt to be a suitable advance. However," he said, "I can see that your position might be different now. I will give you a check for five thousand."

McGregor shook his head. "Ten, or nothing."

Wayne was silent. After several minutes he nodded.

"Ten thousand it is. But I shall expect a strict accounting at the conclusion of the job."

"Of course."

"You will have the check as soon as we land."

The pilot said, "Silverstone up ahead."

———

McGregor peered down as they passed over the house on the promontory. From above, it still appeared huge, and surrounded by a kind of moat of lawn, a swimming pool, a tennis court—all concealed from ground level by a dense ring of palm trees.

They were back over water again. The pilot swung north, moving offshore. McGregor stared down at the water.

"Go as slow as you can," he said.

"You want to stall?" the pilot asked.

"As slow as you can," he repeated.

"Okay, okay."

They were still moving very fast, it seemed. Soon they were a mile out to sea, and he had not seen the ship.

"Go back."

The Piper Cub tilted, turned, and came back. The shadow skittered over the blue waters. McGregor was looking into the water at the oblique angle that provided the best visibility. He watched as the water turned from green-blue to deep blue, then lighter shades as it became more shallow. They crossed the outer reef. They had missed the ship.

"Around. Go back."

"Damn," Wayne said. "It's here someplace."

"Be patient," McGregor said. "If worse comes to worst, we can use an echo sounder."

"Where'll we get that?"

"Kingston."

McGregor stared out the window again. He knew that the *Grave Descend* had gone down farther to the west, but he said nothing. Searching for a sunken ship was supposed to be a long and frustrating business, and it would be best if he made it so.

They continued for another half hour, until the pilot said, "Fuel's getting down."

McGregor said, "Try it a little west."

They did, going out without seeing it. But coming back, as he stared down at the water, he saw the outline of the ship faintly through the blue. It lay at an angle, tipped slightly to port, just beyond the far reef.

"There it is!"

Wayne showed excitement. "Where? Where is it?"

The pilot circled, and they came over it a second time.

"Right"—Wayne nodded—"that's it." He produced a Polaroid camera and snapped several pictures. "No question. That's the *Grave Descend.*"

"Looks like you were right," McGregor said. "From the color of the ocean, it's in sixty to eighty feet."

Even from this height, he could notice the trails of bubbles which still rose from the wreck. Those trails disappeared eighteen to twenty-four hours after sinking; this ship had obviously been down only a few hours. Even if he had not watched the ship being sunk, he would have been suspicious now.

They must think he was a fool.

"Take it back," Wayne said to the pilot, and they started their return to the airfield.

McGregor said little on the flight back. He was thinking about what Wayne was up to. Because, though he thought him a fool, he obviously thought him an important enough fool to spend ten thousand dollars on.

For an aging Jamaica diving bum—McGregor had no illusions about himself—ten thousand dollars was a lot of money. The fact that Wayne had agreed to pay it meant something.

Mostly, it meant that he expected a return on his investment.

What kind of return?

———

At the airstrip, Wayne wrote out the check and said, "Where are you going now?"

McGregor shrugged. "Make the final arrangements. We'll dive at eight tomorrow. Do you want to come along?"

"I think that would be a good idea," Wayne said, nodding.

"Meet us at the main dock at seven forty-five," Mc-Gregor said, and started to walk away.

"There is one other thing . . ."

McGregor stopped, turned back. "Yes?"

"Where are you staying?"

"I've got a little house, east of here, that a friend of mine lets me use when I'm in Ocho."

"I was thinking," Wayne said, "that it might be more convenient for everyone if you were in the hotel."

"It's not necessary—"

"In fact, I took the liberty of making a reservation in your name. It's all paid for, of course."

"Of course." McGregor suppressed a frown, and said, "I think that's a very good idea."

As he walked off, he found himself wondering why Wayne wanted to keep such careful track of him. And that, in turn, made him check behind him as he drove back toward town.

A little white Ford Anglia stuck close, all the way.

6

It was, McGregor recognized, a blind prejudice: he didn't like to be followed. He never had liked it, and he doubted that he'd ever learn. In his rearview mirror on the bike, he watched the Anglia carefully. There was a single person, a native driver.

McGregor stopped for gas, as a little check.

The Anglia pulled off the side of the road a short distance ahead. The driver pretended to look at a map. That was a clumsy gesture, McGregor thought. Anyone born on the island knew it intimately by the time he was old enough to drive.

When his tank was full, he drove on, through the center of town. The Anglia picked up behind him, and let a blue Rover slip between them.

That was not so clumsy. McGregor frowned: perhaps the man knew his business after all. He drove on to the shantytown near the industrial works, turned left, off the road, onto a muddy rut. He climbed up the hillside, bike grunting and sputtering.

The Anglia followed.

This shantytown was partly deserted, with many of the shacks abandoned. The government was erecting subsidized housing a mile down the road; several of the families had already moved. The town was quiet, with little activity except for an occasional chicken in the road, an occasional bawling child, an occasional woman hanging clothes to dry on a ramshackle front porch.

He pulled onto a smaller muddy road, and finally pulled up before a clearly deserted shack. He parked the bike, and went inside. He went in briskly, but once the door was closed, he stopped and waited.

Old houses in the tropics did not remain empty long. In Jamaica, in years past, they had been taken over by the snakes. But there were no more snakes in Jamaica: centuries before, the plantation owners had imported mongooses from India to deal with the snakes. The mongooses had done their job, and more: with no snakes left, they preyed on chickens and an occasional rat.

So there were no snakes in this house. There might be lizards, but that did not bother him. Mostly, it was the spiders. Like everything else on a tropical island, the spiders grew to a fat, lush size; they were quick to take over old houses, deserted barns, abandoned boats along the shore. Practically none could inject enough venom in a bite to kill a man—unless the man was allergic to the venom, which sometimes happened—but they could make you very sick for a week.

McGregor paused inside the door, letting his eyes adjust to the darkness. He saw a large, thick web, white with dew, in one corner; huddled back in the shadows was its owner. Another large black spider the size of his fist skittered across the floor. He stepped on it, and moved to the window.

White Anglia was parking a few yards back down the road. The owner was getting out and moving cautiously toward McGregor's shack.

McGregor turned and moved toward the back. There was, as he had suspected, a rear door. He came into the backyard, littered with tires, beer bottles, old cans, which lay scattered in high wet grass.

He came around the house, and moved down two

others before slipping up to the street. He saw the Anglia, and the driver crouched in front of the shack McGregor had just left.

McGregor waited until the driver began to suspect no one was inside. It was several minutes; the driver was being cautious. Then he went inside.

In an instant, McGregor had moved around to the car, pulled the hood latch, raised it. He found the distributor and began pulling wires. Then, as quietly as he could, he shut the hood, went up to his bike, raised the kickstand, and turning it around, rolled down the hill.

Halfway down, he started the ignition and roared off.

So much, he thought, for tails. Wayne would have to get himself a better boy next time.

And then he began to wonder: what if Wayne hadn't hired this tail?

―

The truck with all the equipment was parked in front of the Cockatoo. McGregor went inside and found Roger Yeoman sitting at a table with Sylvie; Yeoman smiled as McGregor came up. He was a huge muscular man with a calm, thoughtful expression. McGregor had met him ten years before, when Yeoman was just a skinny native kid with a passion for diving. McGregor had watched him grow into a powerful adult and a superb diver; his greatest asset was his calm. In ten years, McGregor had never seen him express anger, or fear, or excitement. Yet there had been plenty of opportunity. McGregor particularly remembered a dive five years before, when Yeoman had shot a moray eel. It was a bad shot, catching the moray too far back from the head to kill it immediately. Angered and wounded, the eel had attacked, gripping Yeoman around the left ankle with razor jaws. That would have been enough to put any diver into a total panic, but Yeoman kept his head, unsheathed his knife from straps on his other leg, and stabbed the moray until it released him.

Later, it took both Yeoman and McGregor to haul the eel to the surface. It was nine feet long, and weighed nearly a hundred pounds.

McGregor also remembered the night when Yeoman had found himself in a bar brawl. Yeoman had a new girl whose affections were apparently contested; around midnight another man arrived with three friends to settle the matter in the middle of the club.

Yeoman had stood up and excused himself.

McGregor had said, "Want some help?"

"Just stand by, man, and keep it fair. Nickies ruins the sport."

Nickies was the local word for switchblades. McGregor stood, but made no move forward. Yeoman turned to the first of the four men and said, "Now what seems to be the hassle?"

And then, abruptly, he swung and caught the man in the mouth. The man fell to the floor and rolled, clutching his face.

Another jumped forward; Yeoman kicked upward and caught him accurately; the man screamed, bent over, and Yeoman kicked him in the face. As he fell, the next sprang from behind. Yeoman ducked, let him slide over his back, and when he fell to the floor kicked him brutally in the stomach.

That left a final man, who had watched the proceedings with astonishment. Now he pulled a knife.

Yeoman blinked impassively. "You want to put that away," he said quietly.

The man hesitated, then turned and ran.

Yeoman quietly turned to the waiter, and gave him five dollars. He nodded to the three men writhing on the floor. "Clean the place up," he said, and sat down at the table again.

McGregor had said, "You didn't waste much time."

"No," Yeoman had said. "In a fight you want to get on with it." And then he had permitted himself a small, quiet smile.

———

As McGregor sat down, Yeoman said, "The stuff's all in the truck. I got the boat."

"Good. Ready for tomorrow?"

"All ready, man. But Sylvie's been telling me—"

"It's all true."

"Hanky-panky," said Yeoman solemnly. It was his word to indicate a wide variety of derangements and interesting activity.

"Looks that way," McGregor said.

"They setting you up for something?"

McGregor nodded.

"Better get out now," Yeoman said. "We don't need no hanky-panky."

"Well, no," McGregor said, and ordered a beer. "But . . ."

"You're curious," Yeoman said.

"Something like that."

"The curious fish," Yeoman said, "gets the hook."

"I know. But we can swim around the bait for a while, and sniff it. We don't have to bite. Besides, they pay well."

He showed them the check for ten thousand.

"Ho, mon," Yeoman said. "That's bait enough, right there."

"Maybe."

"I think," Yeoman said, "that I should make some little investigations. Here and there."

McGregor nodded. Yeoman knew many people on the island, bizarre and unusual characters that a white man could never get to know. His "little investigations" had been useful in the past.

"All right. And set the boat up for seven forty-five. I'm staying at the hotel, as it turns out. They got me a room there."

Sylvie said, "I'm coming."

McGregor shook his head. "I don't think that's a good idea."

She wasn't happy about that, but she accepted it.

Yeoman said, "More hanky-panky?"

"I wouldn't be surprised," McGregor said. He drank his beer and got up to go. "A couple of things you might look into," he said. "Where the boat checked through customs, for one. And for another, who hired somebody in a white Anglia to tail me."

Yeoman nodded.

Sylvie kissed him on the cheek, gave him a mildly

threatening look—warning against hanky-panky—and he left for the hotel.

———

Going back through town, he stopped in the gas station and made a telephone call.

A crisp male voice answered: "Plantation Inn."

McGregor said, "Pan American here. We want to confirm a reservation for Mr. Arthur Wayne. He arrived yesterday and will be staying two weeks, until the twenty-ninth."

"One moment please."

There was a shuffle of papers. When the voice came back on, it was puzzled.

"What was that again?"

"Wayne, Mr. Arthur Wayne."

"I have that, but the reservation?"

"Yesterday through the twenty-ninth. We have him down for—"

"I'll have to check with Mr. Wayne on this," the man said. "There must be some confusion. We show that Mr. Wayne arrived a week ago, and will be checking out in two days."

"I see. Would you confirm that?"

"Yes."

"Call us back. Thanks so much."

He hung up.

So Wayne had been here a week. That was nasty.

And he was leaving in two days.

That was even more nasty.

He drove to the inn, parked, and checked into his room. If the reservations staff had been disapproving in the morning, they were plainly disgusted tonight.

"You have bags, sir?"

"Just under my eyes."

"Ha, ha, sir. The porter will show you to your room."

"I'll find it myself, thanks."

It was a cheerful room, similar to Wayne's overlooking the pool, but facing instead on the tennis courts. He ordered a rum collins, signed for it—why not?—and sat down to think.

———

What did he know?

First, that it was all phony. From start to finish, phony. Wayne had arrived early; the girl and the captain had been no doubt carefully instructed as to what to say. And the yacht had been sunk according to some kind of previous schedule.

Second, he knew that the scheme was expensive. It stank of money: Wayne's ten thousand to McGregor was nothing, compared with the rest of it. You didn't sink a two-million-dollar yacht without a very good and valuable reason. The stakes, whatever they were, must be enormous.

Third, that things seemed to revolve around him. He had been called in, conned, set up. He was very important to the plan.

Whatever it was.

What could it be?

He thought about that for a while, and got nowhere. But he expected to have help soon.

Because that was part of it, he was sure. They had moved him to the hotel to keep an eye on him. But they could do much more now.

They could further convince him.

He sipped the rum drink, settled back, and waited.

———

After an hour, when nothing had happened, he decided he had been too trusting—or perhaps too naive. They were, after all, clever people. They would be more subtle.

He went down to the bar.

Monica Grant was sitting alone in a corner, looking attractive and bored. Every once in a while, one of the studs would wander over; she'd give them the slightest dismissing wave of the hand, and they'd move on. Plantation Inn had a very discreet set of boys.

When McGregor wandered over, she smiled. "Buy you a drink?" she asked.

He smiled and sat down next to her. "Are you allowed to be seen fraternizing with the employees?"

She shrugged. "Probably not."

He ordered two rum collinses. "Why is that?"

She said nothing for a minute, then, "I'm glad you're here. I've been worried."

"Pretty girls shouldn't worry."

"I think something funny is going on," she said. "Wayne talked to me this afternoon. Arthur. He said if the police came around, I was not to talk to them, but send them to him. Don't you think that's funny?"

McGregor thought it was funny. He wondered why she was telling him. She wore a multicolored shift that showed a lot of tan. It was a very even, smooth, attractive tan.

"Another thing he said was that I wasn't supposed to talk to you."

"Oh."

But she just happened to be alone in the bar. He wondered how long she had been waiting.

"At least, not about the *Grave Descend*," she added.

"All right," he said, "let's talk about something else. Let's talk about the owner, Robert Wayne. When did you first meet him?"

Monica took a deep breath. "I never have," she said.

"Oh."

"Listen," she said, "this whole thing is beginning to frighten me. I was working in New York until six weeks ago. Then I got a visit from a guy I'd never seen before, a young, well-dressed guy, who offered me twenty thousand dollars to go on a cruise. It was on the level, this guy said. The owner of the yacht wanted an attractive girl to be a sort of hostess while he took some business associates on a cruise to Aruba. He was an old guy, and all he would want me to do was smile and mix drinks, that kind of stuff. So I agreed."

"I see."

"I didn't really have a choice," she said. "When my husband divorced me last year, he left me with a two-year-old girl. I've been trying to support her . . . It's difficult. Twenty thousand would make it a lot easier."

"Go on."

"So he gave me three thousand dollars, and a plane ticket to West Palm. Return ticket from Aruba. I was going to meet the owner in Jamaica. It seemed peculiar, but as I said, I needed the money."

"So you went."

"Yes. And now all this is happening. I don't understand it." She reached out and touched his hand. "I think Wayne has some kind of plan," she said. "Some kind of very big plan. He's just manipulating everyone, setting up his plan."

"Oh?" McGregor said.

She frowned. "Didn't you sense that? Didn't you sense that it was pretty strange?"

"I had inklings," McGregor said. "But I needed the money too."

She smiled slightly. "Then we have something in common." Her leg touched his, just for a moment.

"So it seems."

"But what are we going to do about it?" she said.

"Play along," McGregor said. "I'll dive tomorrow; we'll know more after that."

"I think it may be dangerous," she said, "for you."

"Yes, it may be."

She took his hand and squeezed it. "I want you to be careful."

"I will," he said.

He leaned over to kiss her cheek, but she turned her lips and gave him a long and resounding kiss.

"This is such a fascinating island," she said. "Will you show me the sights?"

"It would be a pleasure," he said.

"Now?"

"Now."

———

She wore a short robe and smoked a cigarette, standing out on the balcony.

"I've never known any divers before," she said.

"We can hold our breath a long time."

"Yes. A very long time." She smiled. "I don't suppose you've thought of moving to New York?"

"No," he said. "I don't suppose I have."

"That's too bad."

She finished her cigarette, came back into the room, and threw off her robe. She announced she was taking a shower and asked if he wanted to join her; he said no. As soon as he heard the water turn on, he began a swift search of her room.

Purse first.

Cosmetics, eyeshadow, makeup, old letters—and nestled at the bottom, a gold-plated, rhinestone-jeweled derringer. A tiny thing that shot .22 shells.

Very pleasant.

He moved to her suitcase. She didn't need a passport, but she had to have some kind of identification . . .

Beneath frilly underwear, he found it. An airplane ticket from New York City to Montego Bay and return. Made out in the name of Barbara Levett. She had flown in a week before.

And was due to fly out in two days.

"Ouch," he said, staring at the ticket.

Barbara Levett?

That name was somehow familiar, but he couldn't quite place it. He puzzled over it until he heard her turn off the water in the shower. He slipped the ticket back into the suitcase and returned to the bed, where he began dressing.

She was surprised. "You're leaving?"

"It's best."

"But where are you going?"

"Back to my room. I have to make some calls. After all, work starts tomorrow."

"I wish I could induce you—"

"Sorry," he said, and kissed her lightly.

"Tomorrow?"

"Maybe. We'll see."

He gave her another kiss when he was dressed, and left, closing the door behind him. He waited in the hallway, then pressed his ear to the door.

He heard her footsteps, then a click as she picked up the phone. Her voice was slightly muffled through the door, but he could still make out the words.

"Room four-two-three," she said, and waited.

That was Wayne's room.

"Arthur? . . . It's me . . . Yes, yes, just as you said . . . Yes, I'm sure he looked . . . All right . . . Good . . ."

She hung up.

McGregor padded down the hall, feeling cold.

7

In his room, there was a red light glowing next to the phone. He stared at it, and picked up the receiver.

"Sir?" asked the operator.

"There is a red light on in my room."

"That means you have a message, sir."

"Oh."

"One moment, please."

He heard the crackle of shuffling papers.

"Here it is, sir. You are to meet at the Big Bamboo at midnight."

"Meet whom?"

"The message is signed Waldo. No last name."

McGregor nodded. Why not? He glanced at his watch; it was eleven thirty.

"All right, thanks," he said, and hung up.

He went down to the parking lot, where Sylvie's sports car had been left for him, the keys under the seat. As he got behind the wheel, he thought about Monica, or Barbara, or whatever her name was, and felt a little odd.

And now Waldo.

He thought back. He was certain he didn't know anyone named Waldo. Nor, for that matter, did he know anyone who frequented the Big Bamboo. Not your class establishment, but just right for the Waldos of this world.

He drove back into town; the road was dark and at this hour deserted. Earlier in the evening, locals had lined the road on both sides, walking back from work or to bars, but now it was empty, stretching ahead to gentle curves, following the coast . . .

He slammed on the brakes, squealing, as an animal darted out. It was yellow, some kind of large cat. It came to the center of the road and looked at his oncoming car; the eyes glowed bright green in the headlights.

His car came skidding to a stop, and from the bushes, a young girl came running out. She was attractive, as you might expect a young girl to be at midnight, on a deserted road, wearing a sequined miniskirt and blouse.

"Fido!" she shouted, and grabbed the cat. "Bad Fido!"

She cuffed it soundly, and put a leash around its

neck. The cat growled, jaws opening in a lazy yawn, showing rows of large teeth.

"Shut up, Fido!" the girl said, and cuffed it again.

She came over to his car, sequins glinting in the light. "I'm sorry to bother you," she said.

"No bother."

She was classic island stock: high cheekbones, fine features, large soft eyes, hard athletic body.

"Fido isn't feeling well. He hasn't for days. He's been acting up."

Fido growled again at this slur on his behavior. Close up, the cat looked even larger, yellow with dark spots on his fur.

"You hunting for a large mouse?"

"No." She smiled. "Fido is an ocelot."

"Oh," he said.

She paused. "Listen, could you do me a favor?"

He knew it was coming, and hesitated.

"I'm trying to get Fido home. My car isn't working . . . Could you give us a lift?"

McGregor looked again at Fido. Fido looked back and gave another lazy but distinctly unfriendly yawn. From Fido he looked down at his two-passenger sports car, which seemed smaller all the time.

"You needn't worry," she said, going around and

opening the passenger door. "He's housebroken."

"That's reassuring."

"In, Fido!" She held the door open.

Fido jumped in. She pushed him into the small space behind the jump seats. He stood, breathing hotly down McGregor's neck.

"Listen, are you sure—"

"We don't live far away," she said. "I appreciate this very much."

She got into the passenger seat, and crossed her legs, which were brown and very nice.

"He's breathing down my neck," McGregor said.

"That's all right. He does that to everyone. It's his way of being friendly."

"Oh."

"I'm Elaine Marchant," she said, holding out her hand.

"Jim McGregor."

"I appreciate this," she said again. "Just turn around and go back up the road. It's only a few miles."

McGregor did as she said. She lit a cigarette, and seemed perfectly comfortable. But that was understandable; the cat wasn't breathing down *her* neck.

"Actually," she said, as he started to drive once more,

"Fido is new. I had to get him, because of Fiona."

"Fiona?"

"The mate. You can't have just *one* ocelot. Fiona is the lady. Not such a lady: she did a job on Ralph."

"Ralph?"

"Ralph was Fido's predecessor. He was a darling, an absolute darling." Elaine Marchant sighed.

"What happened to him?"

"He made passionate love to Fiona."

"And?"

"Well, you couldn't expect her to do anything else. After all, it's instinct, that reaction."

"What reaction?"

"Fiona bit off his balls," she said.

"Oh."

"That's what females do after intercourse with males."

"Oh."

"In the ocelot species."

"Oh."

"Do you live around here?"

"Kingston," he said.

"What brings you to the Gold Coast?"

"Business."

"You don't look like a businessman," she said.

"I'm not much of one," he said. He was watching the road. "How much farther?"

"Just a couple of miles."

They passed the Plantation Inn on the left. They were going east.

Fido gave a deep-throated growl.

"He just *loves* to travel," Elaine said. "The wind tickles his fur."

"That's nice."

She shifted in the seat, getting comfortable. Her skirt was made of some kind of metal, woven or knit, like chain mail. It made a sound when she moved.

"Do you work around here?" he asked.

"No."

Her tone ended the conversation abruptly. He said nothing for several minutes. They went three or four miles down the coast.

"Much farther?" he asked.

"No. We're almost there." And then she said, "Ocelots are an unusual pet."

"Very unusual."

"I got started with them four years ago. I only had Ralph, at first. He was a dear. So affectionate, so playful. But he began to go crazy."

"I'm sorry to hear that."

"I didn't know what was the matter with him, so I went back to the pet store and asked. They said he was lonely. Ocelots go crazy without sex."

"Oh."

"So I had to get Fiona. I never liked her much."

She stretched casually, and flicked her cigarette out into the night air.

"Why is that?"

"She's bitchy. You know how female cats can be bitchy?"

"Ummm."

"And then, when she did that to poor Ralph, I was furious."

"I can imagine."

"I mean, Ralph was expensive. A good ocelot costs four hundred dollars."

McGregor wondered who supported her little hobby.

"But there was nothing to do," she said. "All alone by herself, Fiona was impossible. She even scratched me here"—she pulled up the short skirt to show reddish lines on her upper thigh—"and that was the last straw. I had to get Fido."

"I see."

"And he's been working out well. He's very good-natured."

McGregor felt the hot, damp panting at his neck. He

certainly hoped he was good-natured. "And well fed?"

"Yes." She laughed. "He really makes you nervous, doesn't he?"

"Just . . . concerned."

"Fido doesn't attack people," she said. "He's quite reluctant to attack people. Robert was disappointed . . ." She let her voice trail off. "You see, we're trying to train him now."

"For what?"

"For a watch-cat. He'll be very good at it soon." Then she said, "Wait! Right here, pull over."

He pulled off the road, and Elaine got out, tugging Fido after her. She thanked him, waved gaily, and crossed the road, walking through heavy gates, up a driveway toward a house that was hidden behind shrubbery and trees.

McGregor noticed the name on the bars of the gate, and frowned.

SILVERSTONE.

———

The Big Bamboo was noisy, raucous, and blatant. He went up to the bar and got the attention of the bartender.

"Waldo here?"

"Who?"

"Waldo."

"Waldo who?" the bartender said, giving him a funny look.

"Just Waldo."

"Who're you?"

"McGregor."

The bartender jerked his thumb. "Back room."

McGregor walked through the cluster of little tables, toward the back. On the stage, a girl was doing a fire dance. All over the Caribbean, little girls with no other talents were employed to do fire dances for the tourists. The girls wore bikinis and pranced around a tray of gasoline, dipping their toes in it, squatting over it, being suggestive with it. McGregor had long since come to the conclusion that Americans had passed a law: no tourist allowed back from the Caribbean without seeing a fire dance.

The rear room was near the restrooms; there was no sign on the door. He knocked, opened it, and went in.

It was dark. Completely pitch black. He ran his hand along the wall, feeling for a light switch.

"Don't," said a voice.

He stopped.

"Just stand very still. What is your name?"

McGregor squinted, trying to see where the voice was coming from. The darkness was impenetrable.

"McGregor."

"Good. I'm glad you came, McGregor. We must have a little talk."

The voice was deep, and wholly unfamiliar.

"I could talk better," McGregor said, "with the lights on."

"I couldn't."

There was a pause. McGregor waited. "All right," he said, "let's talk."

"You are a diver," the voice said.

"Yes."

"Tomorrow you dive off the *Grave Descend*."

"That's right."

"Are you concerned about the dive?"

"I'm always concerned about dives."

The voice gave a heavy sigh. "McGregor, there is no time for sparring. You should be very concerned. Things are not as they seem."

"Oh?"

"Not in the least," the voice said.

"How are they, really?"

"You are being conned," the voice said.

"That's interesting."

"I advise you to get out of it now. Get out altogether."

"And leave the diving to us?" McGregor said.

The voice laughed. It was an unpleasant sound. "Mc-Gregor, they plan to kill you. Do you realize that?"

"No."

"They plan to kill you," the voice repeated. "When they are finished with you."

"I'll keep it in mind."

"Do," the voice said. "Do."

There was a long pause.

"You may go now," the voice said.

McGregor left.

———

Outside, his first thought was to call Harry. Harry was an inspector of police in Kingston, and a moderately good friend. It would be very simple to drop it all in Harry's lap and forget about it. If he had any sense, that was what he would do.

He sighed.

He had no sense.

He drove the car up the road, and parked it out of sight from the club. Then he walked back to the Big Bamboo and hid in the bushes across the street from the entrance. He sat down to wait, and to think, but he did not think much. He was tired; he was diving tomorrow;

more than anything else, he wanted to sleep.

He waited.

A half hour passed, and then an hour. He watched the people leaving the club, but saw nobody he knew.

And then, finally, a white Anglia drove up, with a native driver behind the wheel. It honked once.

And Arthur Wayne, still wearing his three-piece suit, came out of the club, got into the Anglia, and drove off.

McGregor watched the red taillights receding. Damned peculiar, he thought.

He went back to the hotel to sleep.

8

At eight in the morning, they pulled away from the dock and headed out to sea. It was a calm, perfect day; the sky was cloudless, the sun already warm; the sea was placid with the mirrorlike quality it often had in the early morning. Later, the offshore wind would stir up the surface, but now the water was crystalline and smooth.

McGregor checked out the equipment with Roger Yeoman while the others watched. They had four twin-tanks, ninety-four-cubic-feet capacity; they screwed on the pressure gauges and checked the fill, then hooked up the regulators, sucked on them briefly, hearing the hissing of gas and the click of the valves. Satisfied, they turned to the guns.

McGregor used Mantos guns with a midshaft handle. The carbon-dioxide bottles were slung beneath the shaft; a squeeze of the trigger released a burst of gas which fired the spear with a velocity that could not be matched by rubber-powered guns. The spearheads were bulky affairs, which screwed onto the shafts after taking the .357 Magnum cartridges. On impact, the Magnums would explode, driving the shaft deeper and springing out the prongs. A perfect hit, right behind the gills and slightly above, would sever the spinal cord and kill even a large shark rapidly. But McGregor knew from experience that perfect hits were rare. He carried the guns because they made him feel better, not because he seriously expected to kill a shark with ease.

The shark was one of the most successful products of evolution. Like another very successful animal, the clam, it had existed for four hundred million years without much change. It had no bones, only cartilage; it had a thick abrasive skin as sharp as its many rows of teeth; and what it lacked in vision it more than made up for with its acute sense of smell. Studies showed that sharks could be attracted by blood from a distance of half a mile. The marine biologists knew this, but didn't understand it. It was possible to draw sharks by putting a very small quantity of blood—so small that by the time it had diffused over half a mile, individual molecules of blood were widely dispersed indeed.

And besides, the sharks arrived *before* the molecules were dispersed.

Nobody understood that.

Nobody understood, either, why the shark should continue to function after enormous injury. There was talk of a diffuse nervous system; certainly, the brain and cord could be badly damaged—to a degree that would kill a man instantly—without stopping a shark from cheerfully eating you in very large chunks.

He knew they did not die easily.

He also knew that hammerheads were tougher than most. And the *Grave Descend* was sunk in hammerhead country.

As he checked the explosive heads, screwing the shells onto the shaft, Monica said, "Is that really necessary?"

"I'm afraid so."

Arthur Wayne was watching from one side, drinking a beer. In keeping with a day on the water, he had forsaken his suit for bathing trunks and a bright plaid sport shirt.

"You wouldn't advise swimming around on the surface while you dive?" he asked.

"I certainly wouldn't," McGregor said.

Sylvie was setting out the rubber suits, fins, and masks. She came up to McGregor and nodded slightly toward Monica.

"I don't like her," she said.

"Neither do I," McGregor said.

"I don't believe you," she said.

"You should."

———

It took an hour to reach the promontory; they went farther east, passing beyond the far reef, and McGregor climbed to the bridge. They had the Polaroid pictures to help them, but the best way to find a wreck was still to get high on the bridge and look down.

He ordered the boat to slow, and peered over the side. The water was clear today; there had not been a storm for a week; looking down, he could see the shelf of the reef, with waving vegetation, and then the drop-off, sinking into deep blue.

Keeping an eye on the promontory for orientation, it took them half an hour of circling before they found it. The stern, in shallower water, was quite clear. The bow was deeper, lost in blue.

"That's it," McGregor said. The boy on the bow

dropped anchor, counting the stripes on the line as it went over the side.

"How deep?"

"Seventy."

McGregor looked back at Yeoman, who was bent over the stern, peering down with a glass-bottomed tube. He looked back.

"That's it, man."

The engines idled and died. Yeoman began to get into his rubber wet-suit. With Sylvie's help, he shrugged into the heavy twin-tank backpack, pulled the regulator hose around, clipped the strap around his neck, and sucked. There was a loud hiss as he breathed.

McGregor came down from the bridge and pulled on his suit.

Wayne came over. "One last thing," he said. He had a deck plan of the ship in his hands. "We are particularly interested in two things down there. The first is a new sculpture that the owner recently bought. It was put aboard in Naples; it's a modern thing, chrome. He wants it brought up before corrosion sets in. Located here, in the master stateroom." He pointed to the map.

McGregor nodded. "I'll check it."

"The other thing is the safe. It's back here, also in the stateroom. But we can worry about that later."

McGregor said, "Is it big?"

"Not very. Just a little thing."

"What's in it?"

"I don't know," Wayne said. "But my brother wants it back."

"If it's jewels, maybe we can open it and remove the contents—"

"No, he wants it brought up intact."

"All right," McGregor said. "We'll worry about that later, this afternoon."

Yeoman was already stepping clumsily to the stern, breathing through the regulator in hissing gasps, his flippered feet clomping on the deck.

McGregor pulled on his tank, feeling the weight on his back, the cutting pressure of the straps on his shoulder, even through the wet-suit rubber. He tightened his quick-release buckle straps. The tanks were terribly heavy on the surface; underwater, they were much lighter.

He sucked a mouthful of cold, dry air, blew it out, and pulled on his mask. He moved to the stern with Yeoman.

Yeoman nodded, smiled with the regulator between his teeth, put his hand over his mask, and rolled back off the stern. There was a splash. McGregor waited, not looking back, but staring forward at the group on the boat—Sylvie, Monica, and Wayne.

Sylvie looked over the side. "He's down."

She meant that Yeoman was deep enough that McGregor would not hit him rolling off. A man with a hundred-pound tank, ten pounds of weight, and his own body mass sank a good distance in the water.

McGregor nodded, winked at Sylvie through his mask, gripped the glass so that it would not be pulled off as he entered the water, and fell back. His tanks broke the water, and he was down, in a silver swirl of bubbles. He took a breath, the sound of the air and the clicking regulator loud in the water.

He began to descend.

Directly facing him was the stern of the boat, riding in the water. Looking forward, he could see the bow and the anchor line. Yeoman came up; he made a signal with his hands, a flexing of his fist, to indicate he was getting the guns. McGregor waited, hanging quietly at twenty feet, while Yeoman broke surface, his body mirrored from beneath, decapitated, his head above.

McGregor looked down, to the blue beneath him. The *Grave Descend* was directly below, just outside the wall of the far reef, which plunged sharply down from near the surface to almost a hundred feet. The ship lay partly on its side, just as he had seen from the air. No bubbles trailed up from it now.

He looked carefully. A small school of barracuda swam past, and there were jacks, majors, and other tiny fish that moved almost immediately into any wreck, but no sharks.

Not yet.

Yeoman came back, clutching two guns in his hand. He gave one to McGregor, handling it carefully. He pointed to the handle, to indicate that the safety was on. McGregor nodded, and pointed down at the wreck.

They upended, and kicked downward. Though the surface water was warm, as they went down it became colder. McGregor was glad for the wet-suit. He gripped the handle of the gun, feeling the balance.

His depth-gauge showed sixty-two feet as they reached the stern of the *Grave Descend*. As always, whenever he came upon a wreck underwater, he was struck by the size of it. A boat which appeared only moderately large on the surface was huge underwater, when you could see all of it, and were free to swim around it. Yeoman went around, kicking easily, his arms at his sides. McGregor followed him, and they disappeared into the shadows beneath the curve of the stern. The propellers, five feet across, large bronze and polished, were directly ahead. Yeoman checked the shafts while McGregor checked the undersurface of the stern.

It was only a few minutes before he saw the gaping hole, somewhat forward from the stern. It was a large, neat hole which looked as if it had been punched out from within; the metal was torn outward. McGregor ran his fingers lightly over the jagged edge, knowing that human skin in water was fragile; he did not want a cut.

The hole was four feet across. He was easily able to wriggle in, his metal tanks clanging once against the edge. It was dark inside; he flicked on his underwater flashlight and swung the yellow beam around.

The engine room. To the left and right, large twin diesels faced him. He turned the light to the walls of the room, looking for damage, pitting, blacking, the signs of an explosion . . .

There were none, of course. This explosion had been carefully prepared. Its force was directed almost entirely outward, through the hull.

Yeoman appeared at his side, and gestured to indicate that the propellers were all right. McGregor signaled that they should begin looking farther; Yeoman nodded. From the engine room, they swam forward and squeezed through a door, going down a carpeted hallway. The rooms opening off the hall were simple; plain metal bunk beds, lightweight metal dressers. These were the crew's quarters. At the end of the hall, there was a narrow stairs. They kicked up, gliding past the rungs, and came onto the deck. The staterooms were here, and the guest quarters. The walls and doors were polished mahogany.

McGregor, remembering the plan of the ship, moved forward to the main stateroom, opened the door, and went inside. His air burbled up, struck the ceiling, and ran trickling along the roof to the open window, where it climbed to the surface.

He swung the torch around the room. It was elegant, a fitting room for the rest of the yacht. He looked for the sculpture.

He didn't see it.

He looked again, the torch beam sweeping across the floor, in case it had fallen.

There was no chrome sculpture.

Peculiar.

He kicked over to the aft wall, opened a cabinet, and found the safe. It was not large, but firmly bolted down. He gave a tug, then felt beneath the cabinet to the large bolts.

Yeoman came over, and signaled he was going up to the bridge. McGregor nodded and followed. They moved down the deck passage, Yeoman floating above the carpeted floor as he kicked smoothly ahead.

They came out on the stern deck, and clicked off their torches, then swam up to the bridge. They examined the charts and maps which remained on the shelf.

It was then that McGregor heard it.

For a moment, he could not be sure. He signaled to Yeoman to stop breathing for a moment. The two men hung silent in the water, and listened.

There was a low but distinct humming sound.

———

Yeoman gestured with his hands to indicate he thought it was a surface boat far off. McGregor shook his head: outboards didn't sound that way. They were sharper, more a buzzing sound. This was a hum, and it was coming from below.

From the boat.

He kicked down, reentered the deck passage, and slipped forward. Every so often he paused, holding his breath, and waited until the trickling of his bubbles on the roof had died.

Then he would hear the humming sound, fix it, and move toward it.

Yeoman, understanding, had remained on the aft deck. The fewer people inside, where their air would make noise, the better.

McGregor found himself moving to the narrow galley, and still farther toward the bow, into a forward storage room of some sort. It was very dark; the flashlight cut a narrow pale beam in the water.

The humming was loud in this room, very loud. He swung the beam around. There were life preservers floating up against the ceiling; there were oars, canned food, tarps, supplies in a jumble in the room.

And the humming.

He frowned as he moved the beam. He saw something reflect back, and swam closer.

It was a metal box, elaborately sealed and waterproofed, attached to the deck, humming softly. From it, two wires ran off. He followed them forward and came to an amorphous packet, wrapped in several layers of plastic.

McGregor stared. He knew what it was: tetralon, the latest underwater explosive. There were at least fifty pounds of it here. And the small humming box was a radio-controlled detonator.

His first thought was that it was originally intended to explode with the stern charges, thus sinking the ship. But then he had another thought about its purpose. He swam back to Yeoman, and signaled him to surface.

———

Lunch was simple, just sandwiches and soda, but Wayne appeared in a particularly festive mood. At least he did until McGregor said the sculpture wasn't on board.

"What?" Wayne snapped.

"That's right. Not in the stateroom."

"But it must have been."

McGregor shrugged. "You want to go down there and find it yourself?"

"No. I've hired you for that. And I expect you to do what I've hired you for. I want that sculpture."

"It isn't there," McGregor said again.

"It must be. Go back and find it. Search everywhere in the boat. Perhaps the explosion knocked it free; perhaps it's in another stateroom. *Find it.*"

McGregor said, "What's so special about that sculpture?"

Wayne said, "Find it."

McGregor waited for the conversation to turn to

other topics. He expected to be asked about what had happened to the boat, what kind of shape it was in, how easily it could be raised. But he was not asked. It appeared Wayne was no longer bothering with the pretense of interest in raising the ship.

McGregor began to wonder if the ship had been sunk specifically so he could be hired to bring up the sculpture. That sounded crazy, but so did everything else.

Finally, Wayne said, "What about the safe?"

"It's there. Bolted down."

Wayne said, "How big?"

"In the water it won't be bad. Roger and I can get it up without lines. But when it hits the surface . . ."

"The crew can take it from there," Wayne said. "We can rig something up. Get the safe up this afternoon."

"It'll take time."

"Just get it up," Wayne said.

So the safe was important too.

Shortly before the next dive, he managed to go forward with Yeoman and Sylvie, ostensibly to check the anchor line.

Yeoman said, "What was that hum?"

"There's fifty pounds of tetralon forward, primed to go."

Yeoman whistled.

McGregor turned to Sylvie. "It'd be an easy way to finish us off," he said. "The shock wave would crush us, and blow the bow apart. Nobody'd ever put together the pieces." He smiled grimly. "Especially after the hammer-heads got through."

Sylvie said, "Don't go."

McGregor shook his head. "It'll be all right. The thing is radio-controlled. We'll unplug it while we're down."

"And what do you expect me to do, while I wait for you up here?"

"Smile at the nice people," McGregor said, "and be charming."

———

Working together, it took McGregor and Yeoman the better part of forty minutes to unbolt the safe. They also searched the staterooms for the sculpture, but could not find it. Before surfacing, McGregor reconnected the explosive. Then he helped Yeoman carry the safe to the surface, where the others caught it up in a makeshift reinforced net.

Wayne was irritable over the sculpture, but he was clearly excited about the safe. Once it was on the deck, he wiped it dry with a towel and twirled the mechanism.

For a moment, McGregor thought he was going to open it right there in front of them all, but he did not. Instead, he straightened and said, "Mechanism is clear," and walked off.

The boat started back for Ocho. Monica came over to McGregor and said, "Did you see any sharks?"

"No. Lucky." They would almost certainly see some tomorrow.

At that moment there was a rumbling, and the water boiled off the stern. Looking back, McGregor saw a churning on the surface which was unmistakable—the explosive had been set off.

He looked over at Silverstone. He could just barely discern a man walking back into the house.

Wayne came running back to the stern. "What was that?"

"Something happened on the wreck," McGregor said. "The boat may have shifted . . ."

"Go back. We must look. We *must.*"

Wayne directed them back. At his insistence McGregor slipped on mask and snorkel and checked the wreck. Visibility was down to five or six feet now; the sandy bottom had been stirred up by the explosion.

And the boat, he saw, had been very badly damaged, almost beyond recognition.

He surfaced and looked up at Wayne. "Some kind of explosion," he said.

"How is the boat? Is it all right?"

"Can't be sure, the visibility's so bad. But it doesn't look good."

"What do we do?"

"Check in the morning. Things will settle out by then."

McGregor wondered how many other things would settle out by morning.

———

Wayne made no further mention of the sculpture, and when they reached the dock he loaded the safe onto the back of McGregor's pickup. Then he and McGregor drove the truck back to the hotel; the others went on ahead.

McGregor relaxed, drinking a beer as he drove. It was late afternoon; the sun was warm and yellow; he felt the dried salt on his skin and the kind of deep, peaceful exhaustion that always followed a dive.

He was not paying much attention as they approached a vegetable truck, creeping along, pulled way over to the left. McGregor started to pass it.

What happened next was very fast, very smooth,

and very professional. A black sedan pulled out from a side road and blocked their path. McGregor slammed on the brakes as the first of four men, faces distorted by nylon stockings pulled over their heads, jumped out of the sedan, each with a black submachine gun.

McGregor checked the rearview mirror as he slammed the truck into reverse, but he was too slow. A second sedan had already blocked the road from behind.

One man came around to the side of the truck and waggled his gun at McGregor. "Out," he said.

McGregor got out. Wayne followed, with a horrified look on his face. He whispered to McGregor, "We can't let this happen."

"Shut up," McGregor said, staring at the machine gun.

The man with the gun smiled slightly. "Go lie over there by the side of the road. Face down, hands on top of your head."

Two other men had already dropped the tailgate of McGregor's truck, and were wrestling the safe out.

"On your faces," the man said. "Move."

McGregor and Wayne lay down. They heard the men grunting as they lifted the safe, and transferred it to the sedan.

Wayne was silent. McGregor found himself astonished at the complexity of the game being played. From a ship that was sunk a day after it supposedly went down, to scares and maneuvers, and now a planned robbery of the safe. Obviously, Wayne was part of the group; obviously, it was all arranged from the beginning.

It was a show for McGregor's benefit. But what was he supposed to make of it?

Glancing to one side, he saw the men slamming the doors to the sedan as they got in. The first sedan drove off. The other men were piling into the second sedan.

At that moment, Wayne jumped up and ran toward the other sedan. He shouted "Stop!" and then something else before one of the men coolly swung the machine gun, catching him in the stomach, then the head, with the barrel. Wayne slumped; the car drove off.

When it was gone, McGregor went over to Wayne. If it had been a show, it was a good one: Wayne had a huge gash along his left ear, and he was unconscious.

A very good show. Too good, he thought, as he picked Wayne up and gently eased him into the truck.

———

Arthur Wayne regained consciousness in the clinic, while the doctors were sewing up his skull laceration. His first words were: "Did they get it? Did they get away?"

"Don't talk now," the doctor said. "Wait."

"Did they get it?"

"Yes," McGregor said. "They got it."

Wayne groaned. "That ruins everything."

"Don't move," the doctor said. "We're trying to help you."

"Ruined, everything ruined," Wayne said. Then they gave him a shot, and he was quiet.

McGregor went outside. In the deepening dusk, Yeoman was there, with Sylvie.

"What happened?"

"Somebody collected the safe. Very efficient. At least eight men, with machine guns."

Yeoman shook his head. "Professional."

"Extremely. Wayne tried to stop them; he's getting his stitches now."

Yeoman frowned. "Not professional," he said.

"How do you mean?"

"Professionals would have shot him."

"But it wasn't a setup," McGregor said. "It couldn't have been. You could see bare bone where they hit him."

"Maybe it was a mistake."

"You mean they hit him too hard? If that's so, it was a big mistake. Because now it has to be reported."

"We can check," Yeoman said. "Eight submachine

guns will be easy. Which reminds me: I got word on the customs transit for the *Grave Descend*."

"Yes?"

"It never passed customs. Not anywhere. Not in Montego, not in Ocho. The customs people were waiting. They knew about the ship, but they give the captains forty-eight hours offshore before they have to register."

"What do the customs people say now?"

Yeoman shook his head. "You're going to be in trouble. You dove on a ship that hadn't—"

At that moment, light flashing, a police sedan came up. A light-skinned, brisk man got out. "Mr. James Mc-Gregor?"

"Yes," McGregor said.

"I am Inspector Burnham. We'd like to talk to you."

"What about?"

Burnham held open the door to the sedan. "If you please."

McGregor said, "I'm not sure—"

"We are," Burnham said. "Inside. Please."

McGregor got into the car, and they drove off into the soft Jamaican night.

PART II
DARK SWAMP

Being in a ship is being in jail,
with the chance of being drowned.

—SAMUEL JOHNSON

9

Inspector Burnham had a small office decorated by a cheap desk, a rickety chair, a small desk lamp, and a noisy fly which buzzed around the room as they talked.

Inspector Burnham was newly trained at the police academy in Kingston. He was very thorough and conscientious. There was a half hour spent with forms before he began with his questions. He asked McGregor to begin at the beginning, and McGregor did, relating his meeting with Wayne at the Plantation Inn. Occasionally, Burnham would interrupt with a question.

"Who is the owner of the *Grave Descend*?"

"A man named Robert Wayne. Pittsburgh, Pennsylvania."

"We can check on that," Burnham said, writing it down. "Go on."

Some time later Burnham again interrupted.

"What exactly was the nature of this sculpture?"

"I don't know, except that it was put aboard in Naples. And it was modern and heavy."

"Naples?"

"That was the last port of call before West Palm."

"Then the sculpture is Italian?"

"I assume so, but I don't know."

"How large is it?"

"You'd have to ask Wayne. I never saw it."

"You didn't find it when you dove?"

"No."

"That's difficult to believe."

McGregor shrugged. "Go look for yourself."

Burnham smiled thinly. "I think not." He paused to light a cigarette. "How is your Italian history?"

"I've heard of Garibaldi."

"More recently than that," Burnham said.

"Mussolini? I've heard of him too."

"What have you heard?"

"He ran a police state," McGregor said.

Burnham made a clucking sound. "Don't be nasty."

"Ask your question."

"I am curious to know if you have heard of Trevo."

"No."

"It is a town in Sicily."

McGregor shook his head. "No bells."

"A battle was fought there. During the Second World War. A rather large German detachment was wiped out by Italian partisans. The reprisals were fierce."

"And?"

Burnham shrugged. "Just wondered if you might have heard of it."

"No," McGregor said. "And if you're through with your questions—"

"Not entirely," Burnham said. "You see, you are a difficult man for us. You have broken section 423 of the Jamaican Maritime Code relating to salvage of vessels not having passed customs. The Code has never been broken before; the police have always been sufficiently alert to prevent what you have, in fact, done—boarded a sunken vessel and removed ship's articles in unauthorized fashion."

"Embarrassing," McGregor said. "What are you going to do about it?"

"Nothing," Burnham said. "For the moment. Later, we may . . ."

"Think of something?"

"Yes. Think of something."

"I'll look forward to it," McGregor said. "But meantime you may want a statement from Wayne, who was bashed over the head while the safe was being lifted. That might be a nice place for you to begin—"

The telephone rang. Burnham spoke briefly, his face darkening. When he hung up, he said, "It appears Mr. Wayne has no statement for us. The officer interviewing him says he denies any knowledge of a robbery. He says his cut was an accident. He says he stumbled while climbing into your truck."

"Isn't that interesting."

"He also says that no safe was removed from the ship. No article of any kind."

"And you believe him," McGregor said.

"We are reserving judgment."

"Is that the kind of thing they teach you to say in the Kingston academy?"

"They teach us only caution," Burnham said. "Caution and patience."

McGregor got up. "Well, good luck," he said. "With the patient approach."

Burnham watched him. "Don't leave Ocho,"

he said, "without informing us. And don't leave Jamaica."

"I wasn't planning it."

"I'm sure not," Burnham said evenly. As McGregor left, he said, "One last thing."

"Yes?"

"You might find the sculpture, Mr. McGregor."

"Would that help?"

"It would." Burnham nodded. "Because otherwise we might conclude that you had stolen it."

He let McGregor think that over as he walked outside. As soon as he got out, he heard a growl. A deep, threatening, but familiar sound.

He looked over and saw Fido.

Behind Fido, holding him on a thin leash, was Elaine. She had traded her metallic dress for one composed of plastic circles wired together.

"Walking the ocelot?" McGregor asked.

"Yes," she said.

He walked along with her, down the road. He could find a taxi in town, a few hundred yards away. As they walked, Elaine said, "Wasn't that the police building you came out of?"

"It was."

"What were you doing there?"

"Answering a few friendly questions."

"What about?" she asked.

He was going to tell her when everything around him turned a cold and painful shade of black, and he sank to the ground.

10

He was relaxed and peaceful. Nothing bothered him. He was dimly aware of squealing tires and a grinding engine on a mountain road. Then he was aware of a fresh, cool smell from the mountains. And then they were pinching his arm again.

The next thing he noticed was a buzzing sound, like a saw cutting wood. He felt a new kind of motion, and heard splashing. He smelled gasoline and exhaust.

It must be a boat.

There was another pinch of his arm, and a coolness of alcohol. He was about to be concerned, to open his eyes and see what was around him.

But he relaxed again.

A gentle motion, a crunching and a lapping sound—a

rhythmic clicking, and a rhythmic grunting. He was sure, without opening his eyes, that he was in a row-boat. And it was evil-smelling: a damp, rotting, fetid odor was in the air.

He relaxed.

The next thing he knew was a hardness along his back and legs. He was uncomfortable, and rolled over. His cheek touched rough wood. The fetid smell was still there, even stronger now.

He shifted on the hard wood, tried to get comfort-able, and slept again.

He was very, very tired.

‖

He awoke to blackness, with a strange chattering sound which he shortly recognized to be his own teeth. He was cold and shivering; he sat up, rubbing his arms, feeling the night chill.

He looked around.

He was sitting on a crude wooden bed in a small shack. The damp, rotted odor was very powerful as he looked across the room at a single, sputtering candle which flickered as he watched, and died.

Through a window which had once been covered with glass but was now broken and gaping, cold air rushed in. He heard chattering birds outside, and the rustle of wind in trees.

And that smell.

He rubbed his head, which ached exorbitantly, and touched his elbow. It was sore; the sleeve was pulled back; peering closely in the darkness, he saw three red pricks.

Needle marks.

His head throbbed as he stood and walked unsteadily to the window. He looked out on a dense jungle, thickly overgrown, and a muddy clearing around the shack.

He sniffed the air, and saw steam rising into the cold from the mud. And then, abruptly, he knew where he was: the Pit.

The Pit was the local term for a vast swampy marsh in southwestern Jamaica. It was twenty miles across, a wilderness region, known primarily for its value as a hunting ground. Local boatmen brought the tourists up here from Kingston to spend a night hunting the favorite attraction, the crocodile.

McGregor went to the door, which was damp and decaying. He pulled it open and stepped outside.

The Jamaican crocodile was a peculiar and local variety. It seldom grew very long—no more than four or five feet—but what it lacked in size, it made up for in viciousness. Even a small one would attack a man, and many limping locals could testify to the sharpness of the teeth.

The Pit. He sighed.

There were stories of pirate treasure buried here; Morgan supposedly cached gold in the swamp, carrying it by long boat up from Port Royal, the ancient site of modern Kingston. There were stories of millions of dollars in bullion hidden in these swamps. There were also stories of ghosts, men lost and doomed to wander here forever.

McGregor did not believe in ghosts, but he knew it was easy to become lost here. And at night, without any more than a sliver of moon, it would be especially easy. And with the crocodiles . . .

He leaned against the shack.

He would have to wait for morning. There was no chance of moving tonight. He was undoubtedly deep in the swamp; he dimly remembered being moved by car, then motorboat, then dinghy.

He would be foolish to leave before daylight.

He went back inside and sat down, still shivering. He felt like hell. His head ached, he was cold, he was hungry. He looked around the room for food; there was a crumpled-up paper bag in one corner. He opened it slowly, curiously.

And found a compass. Bright, shiny, new.

A compass.

Someone was looking after him. The intention,

clearly, was for him to wait until morning, then use the compass to find his way out of the swamp. That was what he was expected to do. It was what any sensible person would do. He began to think about it. And he decided to stop being sensible.

———

The first mile was hard. He kept stumbling over low branches and exposed roots; his feet were numb and cold, heavy with mud; the wind was chilly and whistling. Once, he fell into the mud and dropped the compass. He spent ten minutes in terror, feeling among the vines and roots for it, but finally came up with it, the glass surface smeared with mud and slime.

He wiped it off on his shirt and went on.

He had chosen a southeast direction, on the assumption that from most places within the swamp, traveling southeast was the fastest way out. Also the safest: going north, one came to the high mountains; going west, the ocean.

He estimated his travel by time. On even ground, a man could walk three to five miles an hour. In the swamp, he gave himself a mile an hour. It had been midnight when he started; dawn would occur at six, and after that he would make better time. But in any event, he would be out several hours earlier than expected.

And that was important. Because if he had not lost a day, and it was still Tuesday, Tuesday night, then on Wednesday Wayne, Monica Grant, and probably several other people would be leaving the island.

He wanted to be around for that. He had, he thought grimly, a few questions.

Two more hours passed, and he began to lose all sense of time and direction. Time was no more than the movement of hands on his watch; direction, the swing of the compass needle. They were meaningless abstractions in a world of mud and screeching birds and a stink and chill dampness.

He pushed on. He was tired and sore and cold, but he pushed on. He came to narrow streams and waded across them, pausing first to listen for the crocodiles; at night they made a peculiar rhythmic thrashing noise as they moved through the water.

At the first few streams he crossed, he was careful. Later he became careless, hardly pausing before he waded in. The activity and life of the jungle seemed to be entirely overhead; the trees were alive with birds, chattering monkeys, and flicking green lizards. But the ground seemed bare and muddy, a wasteland with a canopy of life.

At three o'clock, at the darkest of the night, he was halfway across a waist-deep stream when he realized his mistake. On the far shore, he saw the foliage move, heard a sliding, scraping sound, and then a heavy splash.

It was followed by three more in rapid succession.

McGregor stared stupidly, then turned and ran. The muddy river bottom sucked at his feet, impeding him; looking back, he saw the surface of the river swirl and eddy.

He ran.

It seemed forever to the near side, and then, just as he was stepping out, he felt strong jaws close over his left ankle. Pain shot up his leg.

He pulled his leg onto the bank, stumbling, falling to his knees. The jaws held, but the animal was surprisingly light. Looking back, he saw a tiny croc, no more than a foot and a half, its body scaly and glistening.

He got up and dragged himself forward, back into the jungle. He reached behind and grabbed the animal by its tail, but his fingers slipped off; he grabbed again; the animal struggled with surprising power, but did not release his ankle. He held on, and after a moment the croc let go, twisting back to reach for the offending hand.

At that instant, McGregor flung it away; it went sailing end over end in the air, and slapped onto the water.

He heard a grunting sound. Back on the shore, another croc was waddling up on the bank, huge jaws wide. In the dim light, he could barely discern the shape; it was enormous.

McGregor ran. His ankle was painful and bleeding. He heard the crocodile crash through the underbrush toward him. He ran blindly, dropping the compass, with the sound following him; he knew that a crocodile could move with astonishing speed, if encouraged.

And this one was undoubtedly encouraged.

He ran in a cold sweat, hearing the sound behind him.

And then he heard another sound, in the distance, to his right.

It was the honking of an automobile horn.

12

He felt like a damned fool when he climbed the tree and looked out. He had expected a road—had been hoping for a road.

Instead, he saw a whole village.

Morstown. He knew it well, a tiny cluster of native huts deep in the jungle. It was the starting point for the croc-hunting tourists.

Morstown.

He waited to catch his breath. Then he slowly climbed down, and walked the few hundred yards to the town.

The first man he saw stared at him in horror, then fled. So did the second. He walked into the electric-lighted square; there was a small bar where the men of the town were sitting and drinking.

They all stared, mouths open, as McGregor walked in. He felt his hip, found his wallet was still there. Looking down at himself, he realized the reason for their astonishment: his clothes were torn and caked with mud.

He produced his wallet, removed a dollar bill, soggy with swamp river water, but still recognizable.

"Whiskey," he said.

"Rum," said the bartender, handing him a plain unmarked bottle.

McGregor took a long swallow. It was heavy, homebrewed, incredibly powerful. Heat streaked down to his stomach, and tears came to his eyes.

The natives in the bar continued to stare at him.

McGregor took out two ten-dollar bills, squeezed the water out between his fingers, and set them on the counter.

"Who's taking me to Ocho Rios?"

Nobody moved. The natives stared, unblinking.

He took out another twenty.

"Who's taking me to Ocho Rios?"

This time, he had plenty of offers.

———

The driver of his car apparently spoke English, but McGregor could not understand him. The driver talked a good deal, and McGregor grunted and nodded in the intervals, wherever seemed appropriate; the swamp dialect, lilting and rapid-fire, was impenetrable.

At several points along the journey, the car coughed, shook, and threatened to quit, but by seven in the morning they pulled up in front of the immaculate front entrance to the Plantation Inn. A busboy was hosing down the front tiles as McGregor, the dried, caked mud flaking off him, paid the cab and went into the lobby.

The desk clerk was speechless. McGregor asked for his key, and the man passed it to him without a word.

He took the elevator to his room and unlocked the door; he kicked off his shoes and was suddenly aware of pain in his left ankle, which was swollen and purple beneath the torn sock.

He picked up the telephone. "Desk," a voice answered.

"Send up a doctor, please," McGregor said.

"Sir?"

"I've been bitten."

"Yes, sir. What seems to be the problem?"

"I've been bitten. On the leg."

There was a long, incredulous pause. "Bitten by what, sir?"

"By a crocodile, goddammit."

"Sir, there are no crocodiles at Plantation Inn. Perhaps it was a dog—"

"Send the doctor," McGregor said, and hung up.

He went into the bathroom to wash the mud off. Halfway there, he paused, and returned to the telephone.

"Desk."

"Room service, please."

After a moment, a female voice said, "Room service, good morning."

"Good morning," McGregor said, staring out the window at the early morning sun, breaking above the clouds along the horizon, above the sea. "Send up some breakfast to room four-two-oh. A dozen eggs, scrambled hard, a ham steak, orange juice, toast, and coffee. And four rum collinses."

"I am sorry," the female voice said. "The bar is not open until—"

"Open it," McGregor said. "This is a medical emergency."

The girl said she would try, and McGregor went back to the bathroom, clicked on the light, and paused.

The bathroom was a mess.

There were bits and pieces all over the floor.

He picked one up, and turned it over in his hand. It was a piece of heavy metal, curved chrome, polished on the outer surface. Looking at the other pieces, he had little doubt what he was looking at.

The sculpture.

"Now that's interesting," he said.

There was a knock on the door; that would be room service or the doctor. He opened it.

"Good morning," Inspector Burnham said cheerfully. "May I come in?"

———

McGregor stared at him.

"No," he said.

"Any particular reason?" Burnham asked. "By the way, you're covered with mud."

"That's true."

"I'd be interested to know why."

"Probably you would," McGregor said.

"May I come in?" Burnham said again.

"No," McGregor said. "Not unless you have a warrant."

"Warrant," Burnham repeated, and smiled. "We don't do things that way."

He slipped past McGregor and entered the room. McGregor felt very tired. His foot was aching again. He watched dully as Burnham looked around the room.

"Very pleasant," Burnham said. "What's it costing you?"

"Nothing. Wayne is paying."

"Ah yes. Wayne. The elusive Mr. Wayne."

Burnham walked to the balcony, looked out on the tennis courts, and came back. He stared at the mud on the carpet, then walked up to McGregor and peeled a fleck of mud away from his cheek. He examined it closely, peering at it in the palm of his hand. Then he crumbled it, and sniffed it.

"Most interesting," he said. "This is a variety of clay which comes from the southwestern region of the island. It is particularly rich in alum."

"Elementary, my dear Burnham."

"You have a growth of beard, your clothes are in, uh, disarray, and you appear tired. Further, you walk with a limp."

"Give me a chance," McGregor said, "and I'll tap some cigar ash for you to analyze."

"Ha ha," Burnham said, not smiling. "You have retained your distinctive sense of humor, I see. What were you doing in the Pit?"

"I passed a pleasant evening there, with friends."

"The driver who brought you went straight from here to the police. That is why I am here now. It seems you made quite an impression on the man—they are not accustomed to seeing muddy specters emerge from the swamp in the middle of the night."

"I'm not very used to it myself."

"I expect not," Burnham said. "And your limp?"

McGregor pulled up his trouser leg to show the ankle.

"Quite nasty," Burnham said, bending over to look closely. "But it was only a baby that got you."

"It was large enough, thank you anyway."

"Peculiar. The babies are usually shy."

"This baby had company."

"Ah." Burnham straightened. "You'll want to see a doctor about that, of course."

"Of course."

Burnham started toward the bathroom. "First, you'd better wash up. Best thing you can do to prevent infection."

McGregor said, "After a while. We ought to talk first."

Burnham paused, and came back. McGregor gave a small sigh of relief.

"Talk?"

"Yes."

"But what is there to talk about?" Burnham said. He went back to the bathroom, spent a moment there, and returned. "It seems," he said, "that you are right. We must talk."

In his hand was a small piece of the polished sculpture. "Of course," he said, "you will deny any knowledge of this."

"Of course."

"You were away when it happened."

"Exactly."

"And someone set it up so it would look like you had the sculpture all along."

"Precisely."

"And the intention of that someone was to put you in hot water with the police."

"Undoubtedly."

"Which is, in fact, the case."

"Without question."

"And Mr. Wayne and Miss Grant have checked out of the hotel, and are unavailable for questioning."

"They have flown out of the country."

"Actually not," Burnham said. "We have been watching the airports at Montego and Kingston quite closely. They have not left."

"But they checked out."

"Yes indeed," Burnham said. "Leaving you with this." He held up the piece of sculpture. "Most embarrassing."

"So now you are going to throw me in jail."

"Absolutely," Burnham said.

"Can I have breakfast first?"

"Anything you wish," Burnham said. "There's no rush. You see, you are already in jail."

"I am?"

Burnham nodded. "It will be in all the afternoon papers."

"When was I jailed?"

"An hour ago. You were apprehended in Morstown."

"I see," McGregor said, not seeing. "And what jail?"

"Kingston. Maximum security, of course. You're quite well guarded." Burnham tapped the bit of sculpture with his finger. "I've done all this on my own authority," he said. "It represents quite a considerable risk. But I am prepared to give you forty-eight hours."

"Sporting of you."

"Practical," Burnham said. "We are understaffed, and our workload is heavy."

"So I have forty-eight hours to clear it all up?"

"That is essentially correct."

Room service came with the food and four rum collinses. McGregor handed one to Burnham.

"Sit down," he said. "And talk to me."

———

"I take it," Burnham said as McGregor began to eat the eggs hungrily, "that you are not a poet."

"Not precisely."

"It might have helped you, if you were. The name of the boat, for example—a bizarre name, but a clue in itself. A kind of joke, I suppose. But we must begin everything with Trevo."

"Trevo, Italy," McGregor said.

"Yes. Trevo, Italy. In June of 1944, a detachment of German soldiers with an armored truck entered the mountains of Trevo and passed twelve hours there. On their way out, they were ambushed by Sicilian partisans, and wiped out. It was not until some weeks later that the consequences of this little battle were fully understood. You know General Doermann?"

"No."

"He made a name for himself in the Ethiopian campaign, and rose rapidly through the ranks as the war progressed. Spent all his time in the Mediterranean and North Africa. A little man, by all accounts, nearsighted and clumsy. But clever."

"Go on." McGregor finished the eggs, and began with the toast.

"His cleverness extended to some looting in Ethiopia. Offhand, one would not believe Ethiopia to be a good place to seek booty, but it was. Doermann amassed a considerable private fortune. When the war seemed to be turning against the Axis, he hid it."

"In Trevo."

Burnham nodded. "In Trevo. It represented one of four known Axis treasure caches hidden in Italy during the war. Another is thought to be concealed somewhere in the Dolomites; still another outside Fiesole; and a fourth is rumored to be hidden near Trieste, along the coast north of Venice. Intermittently, some enterprising Italian will go off in search of these treasures. Occasionally, there will be a rumor that one of the treasures has actually been found. Some months ago, the treasure of Trevo was reportedly discovered in the mountains north of the town."

"And you're going to tell me—"

"That it was taken out of the country, from Naples. Yes. The treasure was especially difficult to trace, because it was so small and portable. The other treasures are gold bullion, but Doermann was too clever for that. His treasure, worth a million and a half dollars American, was compact: diamonds."

"Diamonds?" McGregor said, sipping the first of the rum collinses.

"Fine, blue Ethiopian diamonds. And a sprinkling of

star sapphires, for variety. The man who found them was, of course, eliminated by the locals, which in Sicily—"

"The Mafia."

"Presumably. But then there was a small defection within the ranks—a million and a half can turn one's head—and the stones left Mafia hands. They have, of course, been anxious to recover them."

"Where did the stones go?"

"Ah," Burnham said, warming to his subject, "that is a most interesting question. It is primarily a question of distributed wealth. You see, no private individual can suddenly acquire a million and a half dollars without arousing the suspicion of his government. There is the matter of income taxes, corporate taxes—all in all, quite difficult to deal with. A man who suddenly owns a million and a half dollars of anything must be able to account for himself. He must have the proper books, ledgers, stock certificates, and they must go back a considerable period. It must all be legitimate. Otherwise the wealth is useless. Do you follow me?"

"I follow you."

"Now then," Burnham said. "There are, throughout the world, perhaps a dozen men who make it their business to arrange this sort of money matter. They are converters. They take a large lump of illegal gain, and convert it to legal assets. They are able to backdate, to provide old ledgers, to arrange past tax forms, to handle receipts and invoices. They can create a ten-year-old corporation overnight.

"Each of these men does a huge business: several billion dollars a year. The biggest of them all is a Hindu in Bombay, who deals with the opium people. There is another in Hong Kong who does twenty-three billion dollars of business a year. As converters these people take a healthy cut. Usually, it runs thirty percent of the total. A man pays a million in cash from a robbery or a drug-smuggling business, and gets back seven hundred thousand in viable assets. You follow?"

"I follow."

"Of the twelve men, one is in Naples, but he is old, and firmly under the Mafia thumb. Therefore, whoever stole the diamonds would not turn to him. There is another man in Marseilles, and another in Tangier. But neither of these men was contacted. Instead, the money was shipped abroad. It was destined for Venezuela."

"Aboard the *Grave Descend?*"

"Yes. At least, we had heard it was aboard a yacht, and headed for Venezuela. Everybody heard that. Every police agency in the world—and also, presumably, the Mafia."

"Delightful."

"So we had more than a passing interest, you see, in the *Grave Descend*. Particularly since it seemed to be heading for Venezuela. Venezuela is a good place to convert currency. Despite unstable politics, the finances of the country are traditionally good. Venezuelan bolivars are only one notch below Swiss francs, you know."

"I didn't, but go on."

"Our interest became even greater when we investigated the ownership of the yacht. We ought to have known, of course. Everyone commented upon the peculiarity of the name, but no one was able to see the riddle it presented."

"Riddle?"

"Of ownership. There is a Robert Wayne in Pittsburgh, Pennsylvania, USA. He is sixty-five and currently resides in a nursing home after his fifth heart attack. He is quite wealthy, a former steel executive, but has never owned a yacht."

"And Arthur Wayne?"

"Does not exist. Robert has no brothers. And there is no General Marine Insurance Company, either in Chicago or anywhere else. Nor has anyone in New York heard of a Monica Grant. She has never been listed in the telephone book, on the registers of the gas and electric companies, or on the employee lists of any big night-club."

"You've been doing your homework."

Burnham smiled slightly. "As it turns out," he said, "the owner of the yacht is a Jamaican resident, a former American named Robert Levett. Dr. Robert Levett. Now do you understand?"

"No," McGregor said.

"Do you know Dr. Samuel Johnson?"

"Not personally."

Burnham sighed. "In any event," he said, "Robert Levett is one of the twelve men I mentioned earlier. One of the converters. The government knows all about him, naturally."

"Why is he permitted to stay?"

Burnham spread his hands and looked at his fingers. "It is a matter of some delicacy. He is permitted to stay because he tends to invest the money he converts in Jamaican development and industry."

"Ah. Naughty capital is better than none."

"Something like that."

"The plight of the underdeveloped nation."

Burnham shrugged. "It could be worse."

At that moment, the doctor came in and began to

attend to McGregor's leg. He poured stinging iodine over the cuts; McGregor groaned.

Burnham got up and started for the door.

"Wait a minute," McGregor said. "How am I going to find this Levett person?"

"He owns a house east of here," Burnham said. "It's called Silverstone."

13

Yeoman, sitting in the Cockatoo, looked up as McGregor limped in.

"Somebody try to eat you?"

"Yeah. Nearly succeeded."

"You don't look very tasty," Yeoman said. "Where's Sylvie?"

"Sylvie? I don't know."

"I thought she was with you."

"Not me. I was off in the Pit."

"Nice place to visit," Yeoman said. "Who took you there?"

"Apparently, a man named Levett."

Yeoman frowned.

"Something wrong?"

"He's bad news," Yeoman said. "That's what they call him around here: Mr. Bad News."

"Why?"

"He's a money man. Set up the money for you, switch it from black money to white money. You have a robbery, you have a burglary, and you know it's bad news, because Mr. Bad News has your money now, and for thirty percent he's taking care of every little thing."

"What else do you know?"

"He has a woman named Maria Perez. She came in from Puerto Rico, light gal, and changed her name. She collects leopards."

"Ocelots," McGregor said.

"You met her?"

"She was with me when I got hit over the head and shipped to the Pit."

"She's a mean one," Yeoman said.

McGregor said, "She lives in Silverstone with Levett?"

"Yah. In the house. You've seen it?"

"I've seen it. Now what about Sylvie?"

Yeoman shrugged. "Saw her last night, and again early this morning. She was looking for you; we couldn't find you anywhere. She was supposed to meet me here at noon."

McGregor checked his watch. It was now twelve

thirty. It was odd: Sylvie was never late. "Where was she going?"

"Last I heard, she was going to look for you at Silverstone."

"Great," McGregor said, frowning.

They talked for a few minutes more. Yeoman told him everything he knew about the house, which was not much—just that it was large, had a fence that some said was electrified, and some said wasn't, and that some local boys from Port Martin had tried to burgle it once. They had never been seen again.

McGregor said, "I'm going to go there now."

"Alone?"

"Yes."

"That's not wise," Yeoman said, and paid for his beer, and got up.

"I think it's better if I go alone."

"No, man," Yeoman said. "It's better if you don't."

———

Halfway up the mountainside, in a little clearing by the side of the dirt road, they could look out over the paved coast road two hundred feet below, and the coast, and the promontory.

McGregor lay on the ground and peered through binoculars. Silverstone was clearly visible. It was a frame house, but built in the manner of an old plantation dwelling. It was three stories tall, white, with a plain facade and high pillars framing the door. To the left of the house was a tennis court, and to the right, a swimming pool. He was too far away to see the six people who were swimming and splashing in the pool, but one of them, off to the side, sitting in a deck chair, looked like Sylvie.

He told Yeoman.

"What's she doing?"

"Nothing," McGregor said, looking through the binoculars. "Just sitting there."

"Are you sure it's her?"

"No, but I think so."

"Who else?"

"Five other people. I can't really see."

McGregor turned his attention from the pool to the fence. It ran around the house, protecting it from the road, sealing off the promontory. Where it stopped, the sheer face of the promontory cliffs began; the juncture was laced with coils of barbed wire.

"It doesn't look as if they want company."

"No, man."

The promontory extended like a finger into the ocean. Most of it was unfenced; there was no need— the cliff could not be scaled. There was, of course, the series of steps leading down to the beach, but at the top of the steps was a gate and a guard.

McGregor put down the binoculars.

"What you going to do, man?"

"Get in."

"How?"

"I'll drive up to the front gate and introduce myself."

"That's easy," Yeoman said. "How will you get out?"

"If I'm not in the Cockatoo in twelve hours," McGregor said, "with Sylvie with me, I want you to come after me."

"That's not easy," Yeoman said.

"Can you get a gun?"

Yeoman smiled thinly.

"Then get it," McGregor said, "and use it."

"Tall orders from the general," Yeoman said. "You think you command suicide troops?"

"I think," McGregor said, "that you're a smart fella."

"Smart is one thing. Stupid is another."

McGregor looked at him. "Can you do it?"

Yeoman said nothing for a long time. He took the binoculars and surveyed the house, and the promontory. After a time he said, "I could bring the police."

"No."

He continued to peer through the binoculars. "You mind a little blood?"

"Just so it's theirs."

Yeoman put down the binoculars. "Okay," he said. "Twelve hours."

"I'll try to get out myself," McGregor said.

"You do that. Save me trouble."

"I will."

"But in case you don't," Yeoman said, his face bland, "stay cool."

McGregor nodded.

"And if they give you a room, you come and look out."

McGregor nodded. "You thinking of something?"

"A little plan," Yeoman said. "Look out the window for five minutes, and light a cigarette. Then get inside, and stay away from the window. Right?"

"Right."

"Be seeing you," Yeoman said.

———

McGregor drove his truck up to the front of the gate. A native man in khakis stopped him; he was discreetly armed with a pistol in a holster.

"You can't come in here."

"Sure I can," McGregor said.

"You got business?"

"Mr. Levett wants to see me."

"Dr. Levett don't want to see nobody."

McGregor turned off the engine. "Tell him James McGregor is here."

The guard stared at him with open hostility, but went back behind the gate and spoke quietly on a telephone. When he returned, he was more respectful.

"Drive up to the front, park on the left, and go in the front door."

McGregor nodded, and drove along the gravel road until it broadened into a turnabout, in front of the pillars which flanked the front door. He parked next to a Ferrari, a Mercedes sedan, and a white Anglia.

He got out, and knocked on the front door. A maid answered. She had a starched, formal uniform and a taut, formal face. "Mr. McGregor?"

"Yes."

"The doctor will see you in the library. This way, please."

She led him down a hallway to a pair of double doors; opening them, he was ushered into a formal, rather elegant library. At the far end, seated behind a polished teak desk, was an enormous man wearing a Hawaiian print shirt and bathing trunks, peering at a book through half-frame glasses.

"Ah. Mr. McGregor." He stood, raised his massive bulk, his hand extended.

"Dr. Levett, I presume."

Levett chuckled, his huge body quivering beneath the gaudy shirt.

"Nice of you to drop by, McGregor." He waved him to a seat. "Drink?"

"All right."

"I drink only vodka," Levett said, pouring clear liquid from a crystal decanter. "And only Russian vodka. It is by far the most healthful of liquors. Colorless and pure— do you know what goes into Scotch?"

"No," McGregor said. He was handed a glass of vodka without ice.

"Fusel oil, wood extracts, formalin, a little benzene. That is what gives it its color. Bourbon is worse. Rum, though colorless, is wildly impure and exerts a dreadful effect upon the nervous system. It contains paranitrophenol. Quite nasty."

"I see." He looked at his glass. "Might I have some ice?"

"Ice? *Ice?*" He sounded genuinely horrified. "You're joking, surely. Ice cools a beverage to approximately forty-seven degrees Fahrenheit. It arrives in the poor, abused stomach at approximately fifty-two degrees—a full forty-six degrees below body temperature. It is most unkind to your stomach to drink chilled beverages."

"Oh." He watched as Levett raised his glass in a toast, then dutifully swallowed with him. The liquor was smooth, sharp, and stinging.

McGregor blinked back tears and said, "You're a physician, are you?"

"A physician? Heavens no. I deplore sickness: whatever made you think it?"

"They call you a doctor."

"Ah. A harmless affectation. I am a doctor of philosophy. I have a degree in English literature." He gestured to the library. "Do you read much, Mr. McGregor?"

"Not much."

McGregor set his glass down and walked around the room, looking at the titles. One whole section seemed to be about Johnson: *The Short Works of Samuel Johnson*; *Samuel Johnson: a Biography*; *Johnson as a Poet*; *Johnson and His Contemporaries*; *Johnson and London*.

He went to another section, across the room. It was the same. *Samuel Johnson and Mr. Boswell*; *Essays of Johnson*; *Boswell's Life*; *Samuel Johnson—a Critical Appraisal*.

"I *do* read," Levett said. "I am, in fact, an authority."

"On Samuel Johnson?"

"None other. I fancy that I am one of the six or seven people in the world who know more about him than anyone alive."

"This is a hobby?"

"An avocation."

"Charming. But I came on business."

"I'm sure you did. And my business is money, as you know."

"Your business," McGregor said, "is the Trevo diamonds."

For a moment, Levett was silent, and then he smiled. "Good for you," he said. "A remarkable bit of inference." He looked closely at McGregor: "Or did you have help?"

"A little."

"Still, remarkable. And how did you escape from that Kingston jail?"

"I'm afraid the Jamaican police," McGregor said, "are overrated."

"Quite so, quite so. On occasion, I have found myself arriving at the same conclusion. In another context, of course." Levett was silent for a moment. "Why, exactly, did you come to see me?"

"I was framed."

"Oh?"

"Yes. I want to know why."

"You think I framed you?"

McGregor shrugged. "You own the *Grave Descend.*"

Levett chuckled. "So I do."

"I want to know why you set me up."

"That is difficult to answer," Levett said. "It is a lengthy and, I am afraid, ultimately a tiresome story. Shall we go outside?"

Before McGregor could answer, Levett was moving toward a set of doors to the side of the house, throwing them wide. McGregor heard splashing and laughter, and saw the pool.

Levett stood by the door. "After you," he said.

They made a charming little group. In one corner was Wayne, sitting on a deck chair; on his lap, giggling as she sipped a drink, was Monica Grant. In another corner was Elaine, stroking her ocelots.

And finally, there was Sylvie, who looked disgusted and angry.

"I believe you know everyone," Levett said, waving his arm around the pool. "Mr. Wayne really is my brother, Charles Levett. Miss Grant is Barbara Levett, my sister-in-law. Elaine you know—and of course, the charming Sylvie, who dropped by the house earlier today, and was persuaded to stay."

Sylvie said nothing.

"She actually had no choice," Levett said cheerfully. "You see, we needed you. And by keeping her here, we were assured of your eventual arrival."

McGregor looked closely at Sylvie, and saw the faint red welt on her right cheek.

"We kept her outside, so that anyone watching with binoculars could see her at the pool. Did you?"

"Yes."

"And no doubt your trusty friend, the black one Yeoman, is it?—he will be waiting to come to your aid?"

McGregor said nothing.

"As it turns out," Levett said, "we've sent four very strong fellows to take care of him. They won't hurt him badly, but probably he'll spend some time in the hospital."

McGregor did not move. His first thought was that Levett was lying.

"They will no doubt find him at the Cockatoo, and deal with him there," Levett said. "I believe that is where he, ah, hangs out. You must understand it is purely a precautionary measure, intended to permit you to work without interruption."

"Work?"

"Of course." Levett laughed. "Why do you think you were brought here, if not to work?"

"I don't understand—"

"The mob," Levett said, "paid me a visit this morning. They were quite nasty, and went over the house with a thoroughness that was simply appalling. Do you know what they did? They arrived with a fluoroscope gadget— an X-ray. They X-rayed everything. Every room, every object, every mattress and chair and lamp. They were exceedingly thorough. And when they were finished, they were satisfied that I did not have the stones. That is what I maintained all along. You see, I have rather circumspect relations with the mob. Generally, I do private work, but on occasion I work for them. The business in Freeport, in the Bahamas, is one example. So we have superficially cordial relations. How is your drink?"

"Fine," McGregor said. He sipped the warm, stinging liquid to prove it.

"If you want another, speak up. Anyway, we are cordial but not precisely friendly. They know I do outside work. So when it was discovered that my boat, which I had loaned to a friend, was being used to transport the Trevo diamonds . . ."

He shrugged.

"You weren't personally involved in the transport?"

"Dear boy," Levett said, "of course I was. I was hired to convert them, to turn them from black money to white money. Spendable money. I had only one problem."

"The mob was after it."

"Yes indeed. Hot on the trail. So I had to arrange for the money to disappear."

"The safe?"

"Yes, that was part of it. A diversion: we let them steal it. It was empty, of course."

"Of course."

"Once the mob found the safe empty, they would redouble their efforts to find the statue, the sculpture that was loaded on board in Naples."

"Which contained the diamonds."

"Yes."

"And you planted it in my room—"

"Without the diamonds. They were previously removed. But it was enough to put you in a very difficult position with the police."

"I noticed."

"And ultimately, it will put you in an even more difficult position with the mob."

So that was it. The mob would work him over, and they would—

"But I'll tell them," McGregor said. "I'll tell them the whole thing."

"I doubt it very much," Levett said. "Now come along and look at the gear we have for you. You must test it, and so forth. And then you will want to rest—before your dive," Levett said, and chuckled.

14

Sylvie came over while he was checking the tanks and regulator in a corner of the yard. She wore a bikini and looked very sleek and attractive, very French, but her face was serious.

"Are you all right?" she said.

"Yes."

"You are limping."

It was then that he remembered his leg. The bite: underwater, it would begin to bleed again. And the sharks . . .

"It's okay. How'd you end up here?"

"I was looking for you," she said, almost reproachfully. "I was walking around the fence outside when a man grabbed me and pulled me in.

Then they made me wear this"—she touched the bikini—"and sit at the pool. All afternoon. I wasn't allowed to leave. And the other one kept looking at me."

"The other one?"

"Wayne, or whatever his name is."

"Oh?"

"Yes." In a moment of female pleasure, she said, "His wife noticed, and didn't like it."

McGregor continued to check the equipment in silence for a time. Then he set the tanks down.

"Can you," he said, "seduce Wayne?"

Sylvie wrinkled her nose.

"It's important."

She continued to wrinkle her nose.

"It's really important," he said.

"Will it get us out of here?"

"It'll help."

"Then I will see," she said, "what I can do."

At that moment, Levett came back. To McGregor he said, "Your equipment all right?"

"Fine."

"Good. Then come along. You'd better rest until dark."

"I'm diving at night?"

"Indeed you are."

"Where?"

"Near the *Grave Descend*," Levett said.

"What for?"

"The diamonds. Now come along."

As he left, he looked back at Sylvie.

She winked.

———

At seven, just as the sun was setting, they set out from the beach. McGregor, flanked by two husky guards, followed Levett down the stairway cut into the rock; on the beach a boat was pulled up, outboard motor idling.

He climbed aboard with the others; the boatman pushed off, and started out to sea.

They had gone half a mile, and the sky was rapidly darkening when McGregor said, "How do you expect me to find the diamonds?"

Levett chuckled. "They were removed from the yacht," he said, "before it was sunk. The sculpture was taken off, and the jewels were hidden the only place the mob would never think to look." He pointed to the ocean. "Down there."

"But how am I going to find them?"

"You'll use this." Levett produced a small radio receiver, which beeped intermittently. "There is a radio finder attached to the diamonds. This device will lead you right to it. It's waterproofed, of course. So clever, the Japanese. Surprising they lost the war, eh?"

He handed the receiver to McGregor. All the time, the beeps were growing stronger.

"It's really quite simple," Levett said. "The diamonds are hidden in a coral formation in forty feet of water."

"Who put them there?"

"A friend," Levett said.

"Now deceased?" McGregor said.

Levett chuckled. "Don't be paranoid."

"I'm just curious."

The beeps became stronger still, and suddenly doubled in rate.

"Ah," Levett said. "We're above it now."

McGregor looked over the side, but in the early darkness he could see nothing beneath the surface. He checked his watch: seven thirty.

As he shrugged into his tank, he said, "You have a gun?"

"Gun?"

"Spear gun. It's feeding time for the hammerheads."

"Is it now," Levett said, smiling. "Well, you won't be down long."

"I won't be back either, without a gun."

There was a moment of silence. The boat rocked in the gentle evening swell. The only sound was the beeping of the receiver.

Finally, Levett nodded to the boatman, who produced a small gas gun with short spears. McGregor took it, hefted it in his hand, and checked the shaft. It had a .357 Magnum warhead with explosive tines.

"That satisfactory?" Levett said.

"It'll have to do," McGregor said. He held out his hand. "I want two more shafts with heads."

"We haven't got extras."

McGregor shrugged. "Then I don't dive."

There was another silence, then Levett nodded. The boatman gave McGregor two extra shafts with spare heads. McGregor unscrewed the caps and checked the shells, then screwed them onto the shafts, and clipped them to his weight belt.

"Satisfied?" Levett said.

"More or less," McGregor said. He pulled on his mask and fins, sat on the gunwale of the boat, and adjusted the regulator between his teeth. Levett clipped the radio receiver around his neck and handed him a flashlight. McGregor flicked it on, then off, sucked cold air through the mouthpiece and rolled back.

He hit the water, which was surprisingly warm, warmer than the evening air. He turned on his light and saw a cloud of silver bubbles which cleared, rising to the surface.

He waited a moment, then upended, kicking down, following the narrow beam of the flashlight, which was yellow near the source but faded to green and then blue as it went deeper. In the light of the lamp, the thousands of undersea microcreatures shone like dust beneath the water, scattering the light.

As he went down, the water turned colder; he checked his gauge; it was twenty-five feet. His beam had still not reached the bottom. He went down, with the receiver around his neck beeping louder and louder.

The ocean around him was noisy. It was something you noticed on a night dive—the sea was alive with night creatures, eating and clicking with a strange, almost mechanical sound, like a giant bank of electronic relays far off.

He exhaled, the bubbles swirling around his face from the single-hose regulator, and kicked down. Now, faintly, he saw the bottom. There was a reef directly below. In the light of his flashlight, he saw a huge head of brain coral, intricate and convoluted, with a small school of striped sergeant majors swimming over the surface.

The beeping was very loud now, and rapid.

He reached the bottom.

The reef was low, cropping up six feet above a sandy bottom. It was sparse and unattractive, but alive with fish. He swam low, just above the sand, his fins churning up the bottom behind him. Using the beeper, he sought the source of the signals, moving along the edge of the reef. It grew louder and then, almost imperceptibly, softer.

He had missed it. He turned and went back. The sound was louder again.

And then, quite suddenly, the sound changed character, becoming a steady hum, unbroken.

He stopped.

Directly beneath him was a branch-coral formation like a giant hand reaching upward for the surface. To the left was a hole in the coral, perhaps a foot in diameter.

McGregor hung in the water and waited. He did not like sticking his hands into coral pockets. At the very least, you were likely to meet up with a crab; at worst, a moray eel. He had learned long ago that in the hierarchy of things for men to fear in tropical waters, morays were the worst. Barracuda came a far second, and sharks third. The morays grew as long as ten feet, and they were vicious.

He moved back from the hole and shone his light in. Nothing happened; he did not see the telltale angry pink glint of a moray's eyes, nor the whiteness of yawning razor teeth.

Instead, he saw the peculiar milky whiteness of plastic: it was a small bag, attached to a lead weight.

He waited.

He was conscious of hanging suspended in a kind of sphere of light, reflected by dust from the beam. Within that sphere, perhaps six feet across, he could see passably well; beyond, there was nothing but blackness. Anything could be out there. It was one of the terrors of night diving, that blackness, but he had long since grown used to it.

He waited.

Nothing happened inside the hole, and finally he reached in, grasped the plastic bag, and pulled it out. It was surprisingly heavy; he had not expected a million and a half dollars in diamonds to weigh much, but it was several pounds—difficult to estimate exactly in the water.

He was holding it up to the light, trying to see the gems through the heavy plastic, when he *felt* a change in the water around him.

It was nothing he could put his finger on: a sudden change of the current, a change in the sound of fish eating, a new coolness. Whatever it was, it was swift and subtle.

He swung the light around in a circle, seeing only blue water, and then something else.

The tip of a fin.

He came back.

A shark.

It was gliding away, a big one, six feet or more, writhing in that slow, menacing coordinated way that a big shark moved.

The shark passed beyond the range of the light; he waited. After a moment it came back, and on the second run he could see it clearly. The body was normal, the sleek shark outline with the dorsal fin tapering back to a graceful and powerful tail, but it was the head that stopped him. The head was grotesquely flattened, until it looked like a mallet or a hatchet, and the eyes were spread widely, to the tips of the mallet.

Hammerhead.

He looked quickly down at his bandaged ankle. If it were bleeding, in daylight it would appear green, green blood seeping around the white bandage. But in the torch, it would be red.

He looked closely. No gross blood. But it might be bleeding very slightly—

The hammerhead cruised back. One eye, at the end of the hideous stalk, rotated to look at him. McGregor shone the light at the eye, up close, blindingly.

The shark veered away, moving outward with a single powerful stroke of its tail.

He felt suddenly cold. He was in a kind of diver's nightmare—a night dive and a hammerhead. The combination held a fright that was almost elemental; he struggled against panic, against the desire to bolt for the surface, to kick upward, spitting bubbles, exuding fear.

It would be just those circumstances that would most excite the shark, would make it strike. So he waited, breathing gently, forcing himself to relax while he swung the light around, and waited for the shark to return within range of his light.

He felt the gun at his waist, and the extra spears. He could use them, of course, but he didn't want to. He needed them for later.

Instead, he unscrewed the powerheads, removing the points from the spears. He took out the .357 Magnum cartridges and dropped them into his pocket; he threw the points away. He now had three naked blunt spears. They couldn't penetrate anything; if fired close up to a person, they would cause a bruise, but not break the skin.

He began a slow ascent. The shark came back in a

wide, lazy circle; McGregor waited, and it slipped away into darkness.

He continued up, the gun in one hand, the plastic sack in the other. At thirty feet the shark returned and moved close. McGregor waited and fired the first spear. He aimed for the blunt snout.

The spear shot out in a burst of gas; the spear struck and bounced away, but the shark spun off quickly, into the dark.

At fifteen feet, he reappeared. McGregor fired another spear, catching the shark on the side; at impact it slithered away.

McGregor dropped the third spear and kicked for the surface. A moment later he felt strong hands on his shoulders, pulling him into the boat. He was eased out of his tanks and allowed to lie on the deck, gasping for breath, while the motor started up, carrying him back to Silverstone.

PART III
WHITE MONEY

It is better to live rich than to die rich.

—SAMUEL JOHNSON

15

"Nicely done," Levett said, taking the plastic sack of diamonds. "Very nicely done. And now the spears, please."

McGregor shook his head. "You'll have to take them back from the hammerhead."

Levett's eyebrows went up. "You saw a shark?"

"Yes."

"How exciting."

The boat came back toward the beach, near the promontory. Levett signaled to the boatman, who began throwing chunks of meat and garbage off the stern.

"What are you doing?" McGregor said.

"Attracting a crowd," Levett said. Behind the boat the garbage bounced on the surface in the wake. The sharks began to appear, slashing up, grabbing the meat, diving again. There were at least six.

"You needn't be concerned," Levett said, looking at McGregor. "This is only a precaution. We wouldn't want you jumping overboard, and trying to swim away into darkness. Would we?"

"It hadn't entered my mind."

"I'm pleased to hear it." Levett checked his watch. "It is now eight o'clock. Undoubtedly, your friend is at the club. He will be dealt with. That leaves only you and your charming lady friend. We will think of some way to take care of you."

"No hurry," McGregor said.

"Indeed, no hurry." Levett nodded.

———

Roger Yeoman had watched the small boat go out to sea, and had seen McGregor aboard; though the boat was soon lost in the offshore darkness, he had some inkling of what was happening. He had gone back to the Cockatoo for a gun.

The Cockatoo was loud and boisterous as he approached the front door; he went in and spoke to the bartender, saying quietly, "Trouble."

The bartender, mixing a rum drink, did not break his motion as he stirred. "Trouble?"

"Yah, mon. Gun trouble."

"What you want?"

"Forty-five and a rifle."

"When?"

"Now."

The bartender sighed. "You going to need more than that."

"How come?"

"Two boys looking for you tonight. One in the corner, other outside. Bet they got friends."

"How many you bet?"

"Bet four."

"You know them?"

"Never seen none," the bartender said.

"Where they setting for?"

The bartender shrugged. "Out back."

Yeoman nodded. "Point them out."

The bartender nodded to one slim black man in a corner, with a scar along his cheek. "That's all's inside."

"Okay."

"Don't bust up the place, mon," the bartender said as Yeoman walked off.

"Try not."

Yeoman's face was impassive as he walked up to the first man, hunched over a bottle of Red Stripe beer. Yeoman walked up until he was standing directly in front of the table, his fingers resting on the edge of the wood.

"You want to see me?" he said.

The man looked up, surprise in his eyes. "You Yeoman?"

"That's it," Yeoman said. "You got friends?"

The man frowned. "Friends?"

He began to reach under the table. Yeoman, in a single swift motion, slammed the table forward, catching the man in the gut, doubling him over. Yeoman brought his fist down on the man's head, hammering the jaw into the wood.

The man flopped back in his chair; he was bleeding from his lip and obviously groggy. Yeoman stepped behind the table, took the revolver from the man's hand, and hauled him to his feet.

"Where we going?"

"Outside, mon," Yeoman said.

One hand under the man's collar, the other pressing the gun to his spine, Yeoman led the man out the front door. At the door, he paused, and shoved the man out first, into the bright light which formed a pool around the front door.

The man fell, sprawling in the dust.

A second man appeared from the bushes.

"Back, get back," shouted the man on the ground, but he was too late. Yeoman was out, with the gun pointed at the second man.

"Unload," Yeoman said.

The man froze in midstride, then reached in his pocket.

"Slow," Yeoman said.

Very slowly, the man removed his gun, and dropped it on the ground.

"Lots of guns you fellows have," Yeoman said. "Come over here."

The second man came hesitantly closer. When he was near, Yeoman swung the gun in his hand, catching the man across his face. As he fell, Yeoman swung once with his fist to the solar plexus; the man grunted and lay still on the ground.

Yeoman turned back to the first man, who was struggling to his feet. He kicked him in the jaw; the man fell back.

He collected the second gun and slipped around through the bushes to the back of the club. The sound of the steel band inside would have hidden any noise from the front.

In back was a small clearing and a half-dozen garbage cans. Three men used one as a card table. They smoked and played with quiet concentration.

From the bushes, he said, "Hands high. Quick!"

The men stopped, but did not move.

"Hands high."

Slowly, they raised their hands. He stepped out of the bushes. They stared at him curiously, and then, at some unseen signal, they stood and began to move apart, drifting wide.

"Hold it."

They kept going. Soon they would be too wide to cover.

"Hold it now," he said calmly. He was already choosing the one he would shoot. He picked the one on the left, the largest of the three.

They did not stop. He swung and fired, catching one man in the leg. The impact of the shell knocked him off his feet and sent him rolling on the ground.

One of the other two dropped his hands. Yeoman did not hesitate: he shot him in the chest. The man looked surprised as he was lifted bodily in the air, blood spurting over the third man, still standing.

The man on the ground was reaching for his gun.

Yeoman shot him in the head and swung back to the final man.

"You want to play too?"

The man shook his head. If the events of the last few seconds had disturbed him, he gave no sign. His eyes were cold and watchful.

"Turn around."

The man turned. In two strides, Yeoman was upon him, bringing the gun down across the back of his head. The man tumbled; Yeoman collected his gun and those of the others.

He went back into the club and dropped the guns on the bar. To the bartender he said, "Better call the police."

The bartender raised his eyebrows. "Something happen?"

Yeoman realized then that the blaring music had masked the shooting. "A little action out back."

"Who's responsible? The police will ask."

"Damn if I know," Yeoman said, and started out.

"You give the place a bad name," the bartender called, reaching for the phone.

"No worse than usual," Yeoman said.

———

Back in the hills overlooking Silverstone, he felt disgusted and tired. He had kept one revolver, a small .38, but he didn't have a rifle, and he needed one.

He peered through binoculars. The house was lighted, but he could see no one. McGregor had said twelve hours, and Yeoman would give him that. Twelve hours would be midnight. It was now eight forty.

He climbed into his car, and drove down to the road near the house, and waited. In the passenger seat alongside him was a gas spear gun and an explosive powerhead on the shaft.

McGregor, he thought, might be grateful for a little early help.

16

McGregor watched as Levett poured two vodkas, and handed him one. They were alone in the huge library; McGregor had looked for Sylvie, but could not find her.

"I owe you my thanks," Levett said. "You have been extraordinarily helpful."

"It was nothing," McGregor said.

"In a way, I find you fascinating," Levett said. "I shall be sorry to see you go."

"I'm going?"

"Indeed. We have prepared a fitting conclusion for this adventure. You see, the mob has been led a merry chase. But by now, they will recognize that you are the key to it all. They will be searching for you all over the island."

"And they'll find me?"

"Oh yes."

Levett walked to the window and looked out at the pool. McGregor could see that beyond the lighted deck of the pool, near the edge of the cliff, a man with a huge sack was throwing chunks of meat into the water.

Bringing the sharks.

"We must wait for daylight, of course," Levett said. "The tides must be favorable."

"So I'll wash up on the beach?"

"Please," Levett said. "Don't be morbid."

"And Sylvie?"

"I haven't quite decided," Levett said. "She is most charming."

McGregor shook his head. "It won't work, Levett. We'll beat you at this—"

"We?" Levett laughed. "You don't by any chance include Yeoman in all this. Poor fellow: he is lying half dead in a ditch at this very moment."

"I doubt it."

Levett smiled, and sipped his drink. "Every exigency has been anticipated," he said. "Believe me."

A large, heavyset black man entered the room.

"George, show Mr. McGregor to his room, and see that he doesn't leave it."

George nodded. Levett smiled at McGregor. "I would like to talk further with you, Mr. McGregor, but frankly, this is going to be a busy evening for me."

McGregor was led away, up a broad stairway to the second floor. He saw and heard no one; he wondered if Sylvie and the others had been taken away.

George grunted and pushed him into a small room with a bed and chair. A window looked out on the pool.

"Lie down," George said, "and shut up."

George was huge and unfriendly. McGregor lay down and shut up. He lay on the bed and looked at the ceiling and wondered if Levett were right about Yeoman. If Yeoman had been hurt, and Sylvie had indeed been taken away, then McGregor was in serious trouble.

He did not like to think about it.

Eventually, he decided he would have to find out one way or another. He looked over at George, who was lighting a cigarette.

"You got another?"

"Shut up," George said.

"Come on, just a cigarette . . ."

George hesitated, then tossed one to McGregor. He was taking no chances, despite his size advantage. McGregor noticed that George was not armed—but then, he didn't need to be.

McGregor lit the cigarette and tried to inhale without coughing.

"Nice place you got here," he said. He got up and walked to the window, cigarette in his hand.

"Lie down," George said.

"Just want to open the window," McGregor said, opening the window, feeling the coolness of the night. Looking out, he could see the pool directly beneath the window, and beyond, the man still throwing garbage over into the ocean, to keep the sharks around.

McGregor paused there and puffed on the cigarette. It glowed brightly.

"Get away from that window and lie down."

McGregor did not move.

"Get away, I said."

A huge hand grasped his neck and flung him across the room, to the bed. George stayed at the window.

McGregor bolted for the door, twisted the knob in his hand: locked.

George looked back and laughed. "Locked from the outside," he said.

McGregor went back to the bed and sat down. George remained at the window, staring out.

"What were you looking at—"

George stopped talking. He made a gurgling sound, and shuddered. Then he relaxed.

And fell backward into the room.

Protruding from his chest was the shaft of a gas-powered spear gun. The spear had entered the chest and the powerhead had exploded, leaving a gaping hole. There was blood all over the window frame, and all over the floor.

McGregor frowned. Yeoman was out there, all right.

He searched George's body, hunting the keys. No keys. He checked his watch: nine o'clock. He had three hours to get out, and take Sylvie with him.

He tried the door once more. It was solid oak, two hundred years old. He might be able to pull the hinge pins and get it off that way, but it would be noisy, and it would take time.

Another way: he looked out the window at the pool. How deep?

He went back to the door, pressed his ear up against the wood, and listened. There was nobody outside, but faintly he heard a female voice, angry and shouting. It seemed to be coming from some distance—perhaps outside or downstairs.

Back at the window, he heard nothing. The man

throwing garbage finished and walked off, dragging the empty sack behind him.

He waited for several minutes. No one appeared at the pool; the deck was deserted. Also dry—and that presented a problem. If he jumped in, it would make a splash, but if he climbed out immediately, he would wet the deck, and leave a trail . . .

He waited. And then, while he waited, he heard a female voice say, "That dirty bitch!"

McGregor went back to George's body. He took the matches and lit the bedspread and sheets. When they were burning well, he dropped the Magnum spearhead blanks in a corner, and went back to the window.

And jumped.

17

It seemed a long distance, and when he finally hit the water, the splash was unbearably loud. Water was dashed all over the deck.

He hung at the bottom, hooking his fingers through the drain, waiting as long as he could. It was ninety seconds by his wristwatch before he cautiously surfaced, coming up at the side.

When he broke water, he saw no one. He waited, then looked up over the rim. The deck was empty: incredibly, no one had heard or noticed. From where he was, he could look directly into the library, where he saw Levett arguing with Monica Grant, or Barbara Levett.

Barbara seemed quite upset. She was frowning, waving her arms, gesticulating wildly.

McGregor waited, getting his breath. While he waited, he looked up at the window from which he had jumped: the room glowed a soft pink, and smoke was billowing out.

Time to get moving.

He climbed out of the pool, shivering as the cold air struck him, and crawled up to the windows of the library. Close, he could hear the argument more clearly.

"—rid of the bitch," Barbara was saying.

"In good time," Levett said, handing her a drink. Barbara, apparently, rated ice in her vodka.

"I want her out of here."

"I assure you . . ."

"I want her away from Charles."

"Barbara, dear. In good time."

"It can't be soon enough." She gulped the drink.

"You must allow Charles his little adventures."

"The hell I must."

"Barbara, you are being very—"

At that moment, Elaine burst into the room. "There's a fire upstairs," she said. "In the room with George and the diver."

Levett, his huge bulk shaking, strode out of the room. The two women followed. The library was empty.

McGregor opened the glass door, and slipped in.

Upstairs, he heard shouts and running feet. As he looked about, he saw Barbara's purse. It was sitting on the seat of a comfortable, heavy leather chair. Quickly, he opened it and searched through.

The gold derringer was still there. He checked the cartridges: there were six .22s, all there.

He dropped the gun into his pocket. Upstairs, there were shouts and coughs; the smoke was beginning to filter down, curling along the ceiling in a hazy blue band. Three gunshots followed—the blanks going off. There were more shouts.

He went through the doors to the hallway, then paused to listen to the voices. He heard the loud hissing of a fire extinguisher.

If Sylvie were upstairs, she would be down by now. And if she were not—

He ran, back through the rear of the house, to an area he had not been before. He passed servants' quarters and then smelled food: he was coming to the kitchen.

The lights in the kitchen were out. As he entered, he thought he was alone, but then he heard a giggle. Looking across the room, he saw two figures in an embrace.

One was Sylvie. He had no doubt about the other.

He slipped up behind the man and tapped him on

the shoulder. When he turned, McGregor had a brief glimpse of Wayne's startled face just before his fist struck.

Wayne crumpled.

Sylvie regarded him coolly. "You took your time." She spat on the motionless body. "He is a pig."

McGregor took her arm. "No time to be sentimental," he said, and led her outside. The rear lawn was cool and silent; the shouts and cries of the firefighters were muted here.

"All right," McGregor said. He pointed to a path around the side of the house. "Let's get out of here."

At that moment, they heard a growl. McGregor turned and saw two cats in the darkness, bounding into the light.

Fido and Fiona. And behind them was Elaine. She smiled grimly. "Leaving so soon?" she said.

18

Yeoman had seen it all. He had watched the huge black figure topple back as the spear gun hit; a moment later he had seen the fire, and McGregor's body as he jumped to the pool.

He waited then, wondering what to do.

McGregor had specifically said twelve hours. He might not want help until then.

On the other hand, he might not argue.

Yeoman got into his car and drove down to the house. At the gate, he gunned the engine and rolled through, ducking his head as he passed the guard station. It was unnecessary: there was no guard. As he went up the drive, moving very fast, he saw a running figure in khakis.

The guard.

Too late the guard turned back and saw him. He pulled his gun.

Yeoman stepped on the accelerator. A bullet shattered the windshield, and then he felt a shudder as the car struck the guard, bouncing him off the front fender. Yeoman drove on toward the house. As he approached, he saw another guard on the front steps.

With a machine gun.

Bullets shattered his lights and hit the tires; the car swerved crazily and smashed into a palm tree at the side of the road. Stunned, Yeoman crawled out as machine-gun fire raked the car and trees.

He dropped down on the grass, hidden behind the car. There was another burst of machine-gun fire, then silence. He picked up the spear gun and crawled away. There was total silence in the small garden around him. He could not see the front of the house, but he heard a man shouting to another.

He moved quickly toward the side of the house, then looked up. The man at the door was crouched behind a pillar.

He waited. Looking upward he saw that flames were licking out through the open window, and the roof was catching fire.

A moment later blazing shingles began to fall to the ground.

The man at the front looked up and backed away from the pillar.

Yeoman shot the spear gun. There was a hiss of gas, and then the spear caught the gunman, exploding on contact. The man dropped his gun, which clattered down the front steps, and lay still.

Yeoman ran forward, picked up the gun, pointed out at the trees, and squeezed the trigger.

Nothing happened.

He squeezed again. The gun was jammed. Disgusted, he threw it away, pulled the .38 from his belt, opened the door, and ran inside.

———

McGregor twisted away as the first of the cats leaped for him. He felt claws reaching for his back and shoulder; his shirt was torn; the cat grabbed hold, snarling.

He was not prepared for the weight of the animal, which knocked him to the ground. Powerful teeth sank into his arm; he felt streaks of pain.

Twisting, rolling, he saw the second cat moving

closer. McGregor held up the gun to the first cat's head and fired.

The teeth relaxed; the animal fell away.

"Fiona! You've hurt Fiona!" Elaine screamed.

She ran forward, and Sylvie caught her, tripping her and throwing herself on top.

Meanwhile, with a snarl, Fido leaped upon McGregor. McGregor's derringer slipped from his fingers as the cat's jaws gripped his wrist. He howled in pain.

He rolled with the animal, feeling its hot breath, smelling the close animal smells. He tried to shake the cat free, but it was strong and vicious; the claws raked at his chest; his shirt was shredded.

And then suddenly, the cat was gone.

He looked up in surprise.

The cat lay silent and unmoving on the ground. Its head was crushed.

And a familiar voice said, "You want help, man?"

Yeoman came running up. McGregor said, "You must be confident with that thing," pointing to the gun.

"Sure," Yeoman said. "Sure."

He looked over at Elaine and Sylvie, shrieking and scratching.

Without a word, he walked over and pulled the girls apart. Elaine appeared startled in the brief instant before

Yeoman swung the gun down on her head. She settled softly to the ground.

Sylvie kicked her.

"Ugh," Sylvie said. "Disgusting."

"You don't seem to like the company," a voice said behind them. "Pity."

McGregor turned.

Levett, with Barbara at his side, stood at the door. He had a machine gun in his hands.

19

"I have nothing but admiration for your cleverness," Levett said. "You have provided a remarkable diversion. And your friend has considerable resiliency, to say the least."

He turned to Yeoman and fired a single shot. Yeoman twisted and fell, rolling from the light into the darkness of the shrubbery. It was sickening, the way he fell.

McGregor started toward him.

"No," Levett said. "Stay where you are. Otherwise the girl."

There was no movement from the bushes. He could see Yeoman's left foot in the light, twisted in an odd way.

McGregor stopped.

Barbara went to Sylvie, grabbed her by the arm, and led her away. Levett kept his gaze on McGregor. "This way," Levett said, wiggling the barrel toward the pool. "There is not much time."

Burning cinders were falling to the grass from the roof.

"The timetable has been advanced," Levett said. In his hand he held the plastic bag of diamonds. "A problem, but nothing insuperable. It is time now for your final dive, Mr. McGregor."

He looked at McGregor's bleeding scratches from the cat. "The sharks will love you."

McGregor allowed himself to be led around to the side of the house, to the pool, and then to the edge of the cliff. Fifty feet below, in the darkness, he could see the ocean breaking in gentle waves.

He felt nothing but a kind of sickness. Yeoman had been killed; God only knew what would happen to Sylvie.

"Now jump," Levett said. He came close. "If you please."

"No," McGregor said.

"Then I would be forced to shoot you."

"But that would spoil everything," McGregor said.

"I would still do it."

McGregor shrugged. He was tired. He didn't give a damn anymore. He looked down at the water once again.

Anything was better than hitting that water alive. Anything.

"In the leg, I think," Levett said. He lowered the gun to McGregor's leg. "Pleasant journey, Mr. McGregor."

There was a shot.

McGregor, tensed for the impact and pain of the bullet, was startled. Nothing happened to him, but Levett twisted, toppling forward, the bag of diamonds flung into the air where it opened and scattered, the jewels sparkling like stars as they fell into the ocean.

Levett himself gave a groan of pain and fell forward to the ground. He rolled, screaming, and fell off the cliff. His voice gave a final howl of pain.

Then a splash.

Looking back, McGregor saw Yeoman emerge from the shrubbery, a revolver in his hand. Yeoman smiled.

"How you doing, mon?"

"Fine," McGregor said, staring at him. "But I thought you were—"

"Nope," Yeoman said. "Missed entirely. Just a little diversion."

A burning timber came crashing down and fell hissing into the pool.

"But I suggest," Yeoman said, "that we get out of here."

They got out.

20

"I am distressed," Burnham said, watching as the police doctor swabbed iodine on McGregor's back.

"Don't be," McGregor said.

"I would rather you had called the police."

"I thought you were understaffed and overworked."

"Yes, but—"

"I thought I had forty-eight hours."

"True, but—"

"So I took care of it myself."

"That," Burnham said, "is what distresses me. Two men dead at the Cockatoo."

"A brawl."

"Four others dead at Silverstone. And the half-eaten body on the beach, and a fire in the house."

"It could happen to anyone."

"That is difficult to believe."

"Your job," McGregor said, "is to make people believe it. And for the rest, you have two witnesses. Barbara Levett, the sister-in-law of Mr. Bad News. And Elaine."

"That is true," Burnham said. "Two witnesses . . . Or rather, three."

There was a silence.

McGregor said nothing for a long time. Burnham looked at him steadily, and then he said, "Still trying to protect her?"

"No. Not protect, exactly."

"You want to deal with her yourself, perhaps?"

"I don't know," McGregor said.

"But you know about her?"

"I had some suspicions," McGregor said, "from the start. You see, I'm in the phone book, but it still takes time to find me. Particularly that first night: I was at Sylvie's apartment. I was called there. Anyone who knew enough to call me there when I didn't answer my own phone knew quite a bit about me."

"And that was why you went along with the whole scheme?"

"Yes. I had to find out if she was involved."

Burnham nodded.

"But I know now. Everything was too smooth. They knew me, and knew my habits, too well. Someone must have been tipping them."

"And paying her," Burnham said, nodding.

"Don't rub it in."

"Just a fact," Burnham said. "They opened an account for her in Martinique. Fifty thousand dollars—the bequest of a nonexistent uncle in St. Lucia."

"White money," McGregor said.

"Yes."

There was another silence. McGregor shook his head. "She and I will have an interesting conversation."

"I doubt it," Burnham said. "She left on the six o'clock plane this morning."

"For Martinique?"

"Santo Domingo. And from there . . ." Burnham shrugged. "She could go anywhere."

McGregor sipped a rum collins. "You know what?" he said. "Despite everything, I'll miss her."

"I wouldn't," Burnham said. "She would have watched you die, quite calmly."

McGregor said nothing.

"In a way, you know," Burnham said, "the poem was quite appropriate."

"What poem?"

Burnham sighed. "I tried to tell you before. The name of the yacht, the *Grave Descend*, was a riddle disclosing the identity of the owner. Mr. Levett, you see, was a scholar."

"Of Samuel Johnson."

"Yes. Have you read Johnson's poem on the death of Mr. Robert Levett, practitioner of physic?"

"No."

"It's quite well known. The last three lines to the first stanza go:

> *"See Levett to the grave descend,*
> *Officious, innocent, sincere*
> *Of ev'ry friendless name the friend."*

"Charming," McGregor said.

"I thought you'd like it."

———

Yeoman found him at the truck, checking the tanks and regulators.

"What's going on, man?"

"Preparing for a dive."

"Where?"

"Off the promontory. Did you know that there was no reward money for what we did?"

"Yes, but—"

"I feel entitled to a little reward. I told the police that the currents around the promontory are swift and variable."

"Around the promontory? They're peaceful as—"

"Exactly."

Yeoman frowned. "We going hunting?"

McGregor said, "I've been offered half partnership in a hotel on Grand Bahama. I think it's time I took it up."

"And the diving business—"

"All yours," McGregor said. He got into the truck. "Come on. I need capital. We ought to be able to find six or seven of those stones."

Yeoman climbed in beside him.

They drove off, down the road, along the coast of Ocho Rios. After a time Yeoman said, "You miss her?"

"No," McGregor said. "Hell no."